All About Anthrax

Ross Fitzgerald

BLACK SWAN

ALL ABOUT ANTHRAX

A BLACK SWAN BOOK 0 552 99340 9

First publication in Great Britain

PRINTING HISTORY
Black Swan edition published 1989

This book is set in 11/12 pt Mallard by Colset Private Limited, Singapore.

Black Swan Books are published by Transworld Publishers Ltd., 61–63 Uxbridge Road, Ealing, London W5 5SA, in Australia by Transworld Publishers (Australia) Pty. Ltd., 15–23 Helles Avenue, Moorebank, NSW 2170, and in New Zealand by Transworld Publishers (N.Z.) Ltd., Cnr. Moselle and Waipareira Avenues, Henderson, Auckland.

Made and printed in Great Britain by The Guernsey Press Co. Ltd., Guernsey, Channel Islands.

For Norton Hobson, in Melbourne

These tales with some modifications, have appeared in *Adelaide Review*, *Aspect*, *Cane Toad Times*, *Compass*, *Inprint*, *Matilda*, *Nepean Review*, *Overland*, *Quadrant*, *Siccum*, *Social Alternatives*, and *Westerly*.
Together they form an acrostic.
Historical material for 'Another's Trouble' is derived from 19th and 20th century sources, including Geoffrey Hutton's *Adam Lindsay Gordon: the Man and the Myth*, London, Faber, 1978 and Richard Douglas Jordan, 'Adam Lindsay Gordon: The Australian Poet', *Westerly*, vol. 30, no. 2, June 1985, pp. 45–56

Ross Fitzgerald

Contents

I

I look in the mirror and what do I see?
I see a person much like me.
                              Nursery Rhyme

An Ordinary Childhood

Then I must that night go in search of one
unknown before but recognized on sight
Whose touch, expedient or miracle,
stays panic in me and arrests my flight.

Tennessee Williams

Rodney Poole was an only child. Where I lived that explained a lot. Economically and culturally the Pooles were above us. Ormond Poole was a plumber who had started on his own and worked himself up. When Rodney was nine, Mr Poole had four men. At the SEC where my Dad worked he still wore blue overalls – that was a big difference. Thin Mr Poole walked with a cane and wore black hornrimmed glasses. He had a hawk nose and a bent spine which was getting worse. To me he looked like the mad scientist from *Captain Marvel*. Not just to me but it seemed to Rodney as well who screamed whenever his father tried to touch him, which happened far too frequently my Mother said. For his age Rodney was rather small.

Verna Poole, who played the violin even after she had had her breast removed, was scrupulous about Rodney's personal hygiene and his piano practice. While Rodney wasn't allowed to play with me, we did play next to each other, separated by the small wooden fence that in turn separated our respective homes in Hancock Street, South Caulfield. Rodney was often called to the piano. I knew he hated it because I could see him rigid in the bay window performing like a showpiece, while Dad and I played French cricket on our front lawn. Poor Rodney had to practise his scales over and over again.

Though the houses looked the same there were important differences between us. The Pooles had dinner at seven. We had tea at five. They were all Methodists while Dad was a lapsed Catholic and Avis, my mother, had doubts. Most important of all, Ormond had been to Japan and seen Mt Fuji. One Christmas we were invited in to see the slides twice. Mr Poole got ideas from a conference in Tokyo and won a contract with a woollen mill when he returned to Melbourne. That was how he increased his men.

One Friday night, just before the umpire called bad light, all the Pooles were dressed up as Orm backed out the black Pontiac.

'We're going to the opera, Mr Everest,' called young Rodney, ignoring a reproof from Verna. Opera, like ballet, was a dirty word to my father, just like the *Sporting Globe* was to Mr Poole. 'That boy's not normal, son,' confided Dad as he bowled me round my legs. 'Why?' I asked as always. 'It's a secret,' said my father in the serious voice he reserved for talk of Mr Santamaria and the DLP. 'A secret.'

For tea we had the flake and chips and potato cakes that Dad and I brought back in the Hillman Minx, wrapped in a blanket that I held on my knees. After grace we listened to the radio and Avis talked about *On The Beach* which was being made in Melbourne then.

'Why isn't Roddie normal Dad?' I blurted during a lull in the conversation. After a long and studied look at Mother, who nodded slightly, Dad announced very slowly, 'He sleeps with a pumpkin.' I nearly swallowed my piece of flake. That *was* a secret.

'The child must be starved of love,' Avis responded immediately.

'It's worse than a doll,' said Dad, looking meaningful. All of this had great import, as I was still sleeping with Snowy, a toy dog that Uncle Jack had reputedly made in

12

Changi. Dad was trying to get me to give Snowy away to a little boy down the street who didn't have any toy animals of his own.

'He calls it Pummy,' said Dad without a smile. 'Pummy the Pumpkin.'

'Yes,' added Mother in a hurry. 'Every so often Ormond and Verna have to go to the markets to get a pumpkin that looks like Pummy . . . It's the way of pumpkins to go off,' she explained passing Dad another potato cake. I had seldom heard my parents say so much to each other.

'Imagine Orm and Verna sorting through the fruit and vegie stalls until they find a pumpkin exactly like Pummy. You'd look such a fool, wouldn't you Bill? How could you explain *that* to the barrow man?'

'Doesn't Rodney know that it's a different pumpkin?' I asked with big wide eyes. 'He never seems to know,' answered Avis. 'Does he Bill?' 'Perhaps he doesn't let on,' Dad said thoughtfully. I had a feeling Dad was giving him the benefit of the doubt.

'Now don't you tell anyone, young Grafton,' said Mother looking me straight in the eyes. 'And don't you *dare* mention to Rodney that you know about Pummy the Pumpkin.'

I promised earnestly.

'It's a secret,' repeated Dad. I was so excited I could hardly eat the big helping of tinned peaches and ice-cream that Dad and I had for dessert. In case there was anything else to learn I helped with the washing up instead of going straight to the toilet after tea.

I never actually saw Pummy but Rodney Poole took on a very different aura for me from then on. What did he *do* with the pumpkin? Did he still sleep with it I wondered as our school years rolled on. After we both left Gardenvale Central, Rodney had an added air of mystery. While I trudged wearily in to Forest Hill High, an institution for Latin speakers and bright boys only, Rodney went nearby to Brighton Tech, reputedly a place of lust and carnage where girls attended. For the second

13

half of his first year there Rodney was sent as an Exchange student to America. He mailed us a postcard of Washington Square a week before he returned.

One night after tea when Ormond and Verna were out, he invited me in to see his Perry Como Jacket. It was red and white: South Melbourne colours. The team that finished bottom. Once I was in his bedroom Rodney proudly put on his Perry Como Jacket, showed me a picture of his crewcutted American friend, and took off my pants. Then he slipped off his own. Laying on his bed, me kneeling above him, he pulled us both off extremely slowly, using vaseline on the palm of his right hand, our cocks touching, not saying a word. After, he wiped up meticulously with a hankie. From then on he always borrowed mine, which seemed unfair. Once a week, every Tuesday, this ritual took place. Soon he dispensed with the Perry Como Jacket, but his friend's photo always smiled from the bedstead. I said thank you afterwards, but Rodney never said a word. Graeme Manager, the sad Seventh Day Adventist boy from across the road who couldn't play cricket on Saturdays, used to go into Rodney's house at the same time but on Thursdays. Although I'd been told never to look a gift horse in the mouth, I felt a little piqued at that.

The Christmas that Rodney turned fourteen, he was away at Monbulk on a senior scout's camp when bushfires hit the Dandenongs. Being a dutiful son he rang home as soon as he could, to tell his parents he was safe. 'Your mother's dead,' Mr Poole was reputed to have announced on the phone.

'It was a bit tough telling the lad on the telephone,' Dad repeated for days. 'Especially after the trauma of the bushfire.'

I knew much about trauma myself having been placed in a garbage bin by Avis six years earlier and told I'd be taken away to the incinerator which burnt all the district's rubbish. I couldn't talk for a week.

'The boy's been traumatized,' Dr Noad said. Not unnaturally, I wondered what would happen to Rodney when he returned. 'He should have had more sense,' said Dad across the other fence to Mr Rawlings the Baptist, to whom he seldom spoke. Bald Mr Rawlings nodded. In fact all the neighbours agreed Mr Poole should have broken the news a lot more gently. After he came home Rodney went very quiet. Nothing much seemed to happen, but on looking back the street agreed that it was only after the news that Rodney turned strange.

The strangeness first made itself known at the wedding of Ormond and the new Mrs Poole. The celebration happened six months after Verna's death – a little soon my mother said, though she and Dad accepted the invitation. Rodney, who had taken sick during the ceremony, arrived drunk at the reception, held at home, with Sid Poole, Orm's dissolute elder brother who looked like Groucho Marx. Rodney and Sid drank whiskey in the street and, arms round each other, sang 'Friggin in the Rigging'. Then they embraced each other on the nature strip.

Beryl, the new Mrs Poole, tried very hard to please Roddie. They built him a special room out the back with black venetians and, when he left school early, sent him away on a cruise. Try as hard as she could, they just didn't get on. After Roddie got more and more morose, Orm even made him his apprentice, but that didn't help at all. Rodney came home inebriated at all times of the day and night, at first with different chaps but then mostly with a fat policeman called Trevor. 'It's a disgrace,' my father said. There was no need for innuendos. Everyone knew what was going on. Mr Sherwin, the truck-driver who sometimes parked his semi across the road, told Dad he saw them at Luna Park holding hands on the dodgems. When we went for a Sunday swim we saw them walking down the promenade near Middle Brighton Pier. Trevor was still in uniform.

One night there was a terrible fight outside the Pooles' and I knew the affair was over. Rodney locked himself in his room and was drunk for a fortnight. After that he lost a lot of weight; clumps of his hair fell out. For a reason that I could never quite fathom he seemed strangely fond of Mum. Sometimes when Ormond and Beryl were out he'd pop in quietly and see her. 'What *do* you want to do with your life, Rodney?' I overheard Avis say. It was a question she often asked me. 'I want to be a sailor, Mrs E., and see the world, but Dad won't let me.' Rodney broke down and cried. Avis, who seldom drank herself, got him a small sherry from the living room and then put the decanter away. 'It's a terrible shame,' she said after Rodney left. 'For his mother's sake I'll have to go in and have a word to his father.' Since the death our families had become quite close.

Because of his height, Rodney only just made it into the Navy. But having got in he seemed extremely happy. Every three months or so, when he was back from manoeuvres, Rodney would come home alone and sober in his neat sailor-blue suit and stay for an untroubled day or two. He told Mum he'd gone on the wagon for keeps. Within a year he became a Leading Hand. Soon the street accepted him. On Coral Sea Day he took Mum and Dad and Mr and Mrs Sherwin over the ship. Dad and Len Sherwin agreed Rodney had finally found his niche.

Everything went well until Beryl's fortieth birthday which coincided with the third anniversary of Verna's death. Rodney had been away in Tokyo for the others, but this time he was back in port. As it was difficult to combine a celebration and the paying of respects, the Pooles divided the day into two. Although they set aside mid-morning for the cemetery, they couldn't find Verna's plot at all. After an hour, Orm decided to call it a day, but Rodney broke into a tantrum. Floral tributes in hand, Roddie took Mr Poole's car and raced down to the Terminus. He drank like a man possessed. The police said it was an accident but after only drinking for an hour he drove top speed down Nepean Highway, straight into Tommy Bent's statue. Orm's Pontiac slewed off into Friend and Hellier's, the scrap metal dealers across the road. It was a total write-off. Rodney broke both legs and an arm and whiplashed his spine.

After being on the critical list for a week they kept him in hospital for six months, most of it in traction. Despite the strain, Mum went in and visited him every week. He wouldn't see Ormond and Beryl at all. For a long time he was very depressed, but with Avis' help Rodney slowly began to walk again. He even started looking forward to going back to sea and having a little flat of his own. It wasn't all smooth sailing. Some of his fairweather friends brought in booze until the charge sister caught them. After that he was taken off sleeping tablets as well. 'If you want to succeed in life, you've got to have nothing in your blood but blood,' the sister said.

It was only after Roddie got back on his feet that they broke the terrible news to him. He'd been shortened. And because he'd been shortened they wouldn't take him back into the Navy. The authorities were adamant. The minimum for a Leading Hand was 5' 6". Rodney was now 5' 5".

The day he was discharged Roddie got drunk. 'I won't go back to her,' Rodney screamed hysterically, so Mum helped him move into a little room in Elsternwick, next to a pub. A fortnight later she took him some broth. It was pitiful. Although it was the day after his pension cheque, he didn't even have a Vegemite sandwich. Dirty underpants and empty claret flagons littered the floor; little bottles of eau de cologne and essence of lemon lay on the bed. He looked like a dehydrated match. Suddenly you could see his father in him.

'How's Rodney?' I asked last week.

'It's tragic,' Avis said. 'Tragic. Eat your tea.'

The Date

It was Orientation Week and Grafton needed heroes. He smoked a midget cigar and clutched a book on Modigliani. No one looked at him. Masking his fear with what he hoped was a cosmic smile, he threaded his way to the Library. Books, bound and sinister, pressed in; the air-conditioning made him claustrophobic. All those words on all those shelves! He could hardly breathe. Wanting to pee, he asked for the lavatory. Leaning against his trolley, the attendant leered, pointing down the rows into the distance. Grafton stumbled on. Hidden among History he saw him: Paul was sitting alone, surrounded by papers, hunched over a reading-machine, looking worried and hung-up, stained fingers tugging his tousled hair and half-formed beard. Grafton walked up, hands outstretched, 'My name's Everest ... I got four Firsts in Matric. Can I help you?' Paul looked up, held his hands and said, 'That's interesting. I got a First in Modern History, and a First in Ancient History, and a First in Economics and the Exhibition in Geography – that's the top of the State.' Grafton laughed and fell in love with him.

Paul was an artist. He'd had exhibitions of his work around Melbourne and was held to be Very Promising. The Captain Moonlight Series, the Phoenix Series, a number of Self Portraits. Grafton thought he was marvellous. He used to sit in Paul's room and mix his palettes and eat peanuts because they were good for the brain. All through the night he'd bring him claret, change his records and watch him paint. Paul treated him like crap

18

the whole of freshman year. Promising they'd go away
to India together, then saying he wouldn't take him.
Making out Grafton was clumsy and that asthma was a
weakness. Paul didn't know how much Grafton loved
him, or how cruelly he treated him. Grafton tried so hard
to please. On his birthday he brought him dahlias and
Dylan's new LP. Paul said not to be silly and under-
graduate, but for Grafton their love was real. They
never had it off together.

At a Labour Club Conference at Warburton when
Paul was very drunk he asked Grafton to go to bed with
him. The first-year results had just come out. Grafton
had beaten Paul and topped every subject. As always,
Paul had tried to bring him down in front of the others.
He made out that Grafton had taken him for a ride and
sucked his brains. Everyone else had gone to bed; the
mulled claret and stale cigarette smell hung in the air;
the grass outside the guesthouse glistened. Grafton put
his arm around Paul and, for a reason he didn't really
understand, said he thought they'd better not. Paul
pulled free and stormed off to his room. Grafton stayed
up all night and walked the township in the rain. He felt
stranded like a sailor.

Bill Rigby was a friend of Paul's. Paul had four free
tickets to the End-of-Term Ball, and he arranged for Bill
and two girls to go with Grafton. It was Grafton's first
ball and he couldn't dance. Grafton and Bill had never
met. Still the seeker waited expectantly in an old dinner
jacket borrowed from the Professor of History. Grafton
couldn't explain why he felt so excited, but he did. He
could hardly eat his tea. Bill arrived beautiful and very
grand. He was driving Paul's VW. When Grafton opened
the door Bill was wearing black velvet and a white
carnation. His skin shone like marble. He looked so
handsome, bones and face so fine, that Grafton had to
turn away. When he saw his eyes, blue and focused in
the distance, he knew. He knew that Bill knew too. Bill
wouldn't come inside. He was well prepared.

Grafton's father was a Fitter and Turner who had

19

played in the ruck for Richmond. He was a very clumsy man. Grafton was embarrassed by his lack of education and ashamed of the way he spoke. His father neither drank nor smoked. That didn't impress Grafton one bit. Mother Everest was a small mousey woman who had once worked in a shoe shop. Grafton was the only egg in her basket. She suspected he was a golden one. Whenever she thought her boy had been naughty she'd say, 'Look me straight in the eyes Grafton'. Even if he'd done nothing wrong he never ever could. He couldn't see the colour of her eyes. All that house history flickered as Grafton climbed down the stairs. He blinked. Bill was still there, waiting. Grafton warmed again. Mother and Dad waved the boys goodbye from the verandah.

Paul's VW floated along the Boulevarde like a Porsche, the windows were open, their scarves flapped in the breeze, the air was warm. Bill's voice caressed him as they drove. Grafton felt so proud. Then it dawned. Paul had set everything up knowing what would happen. Grafton dwelt on that for a second and accepted it. He wondered whether it was Paul's way of giving in, by proxy.

They picked up the girls. Grafton and Bill sat in front, the girls in the back, redundant. Grafton had no idea who he took or what she looked like or what she said. She could have been the carwash attendant or a tattooed machinist for all he noticed. All night he only had eyes for Bill. Grafton seldom moved from the table. He drank and watched and soaked Bill up. After each number Bill would come back with one girl to replace the other who sat dumb and numb beside him. Then the boys would toast each other and the dancing would begin again. Bill danced divinely. First with one, then the other. The girls were faceless, interchangeable. Their perfume and small talk, dresses and dreamy eyes were all in vain. The girls sensed something was happening. But the language they couldn't place. They felt dissociated, barred from the network of gesture and sign. Inarticulately they knew they were intruders.

Grafton drank contentedly. He poured another drink for Bill. The waiter watched. The watcher waited.

They took the girls home at midnight. 'Now Shall We' chimed the bells. Nothing needed to be said; the only question was where they'd go. Bill drove towards the beach. Grafton redirected him. The car cruised through the streets and stopped near Lancox Park, the park of his youth. The black swans still glided on the lake past the weeping willows in the moonlight. The public toilet was there too, newly painted. The old man without teeth, a tram conductor, had vanished long ago. Near the Chapel of Our Lady, Queen of the World, the mad girls from Marillac and their Sisters of Mercy slept in peace. The clasped-hands Madonna watched over them; and over Bill and Grafton too. The boys sat quietly, cuddling each other, rejoicing in the dark. They got out of the car and walked down the path, holding hands, towards Grafton's old Primary School. *Gardenvale State 3897* was still etched in brickwork on the walls. The moon was full; everything seemed so clear and crisp and radiant. They had drunk themselves sober. Grafton jumped the fence and went into the boy's shelter shed – to the place where he'd sat so lonely so many years ago. Bill followed. The empty, awful times, being odd one out and laughed at flashed back in Grafton's head. Bill was holding him. The fear had gone. They cradled and touched and explored each other in the moonlight. Grafton had never felt so warm. They kissed and lay on the ground and made love each to each. Grafton thought, momentarily, of Mother. He wondered whether she'd know. This time he didn't care.

Their bodies shimmered like silver and they rippled and sang into each other, wave upon wave. They lay there, beautiful boys at sea, abandoned in their loveliness and their light, and they held each other tight and cried. They lay softly there a long, long time. Grafton fell into a sound and peaceful sleep. In his undulations he danced and dreamed. Bill kissed him into consciousness and again and again caressed him and got him hard.

21

They lay down with each other once more and drew themselves into each other in a joyful, hungry way. Grafton orbited like a galaxy and fell soft as moonbeams. Bill took him by the hand and walked him home and kissed him goodnight at dawn.

On Christmas Eve Paul arrived at Grafton's house, hands full of flowers. He gave them to Avis, but Grafton knew they were for him. Something had changed. Grafton saw a softness he had never seen before. Paul wished Mrs Everest a Merry Christmas and negotiated Grafton into the street. Bill was in the Volkswagen, smiling. Grafton's heart sank. Bill leant over the bucket seat and kissed him on the mouth. Paul held the door open and Grafton got in back with Bill. Paul didn't mind at all. He drove past the sand dunes and tea-tree scrub, a guitar and three flagons beside him, and stopped at the beach near Middle Brighton Pier. Grafton lay in Bill's lap looking out to sea; fishing boats were rocking in the bay. Paul stood up like a troubadour serenading and sang 'House of the Rising Sun'. They passed the Chablis around until one of the flagons was empty. The boys walked slowly down the wharf, Paul leading, past the courting couples and solitary Italian fisherman, skipping pebbles off the waves. At the end of the jetty they came to a lighthouse. The tide was out. They clambered across the rotting boards and rocks strewn with mussel shells and starfish, climbed into the little structure at the jetty's end and settled down for the night. There was just room enough for three. They sat and drank the wine.

Grafton sang 'Sad Eyed Lady of the Lowlands' and 'Mary Hamilton'. He knew them off by heart. Dirges were his speciality. Not to be outdone, Paul recited 'The Ancient Mariner' word for word. A porpoise surfaced like a submarine and sank back into the sea. While the ocean rocked them and the harbour gulls wheeled, ruffling the waves, Paul and Grafton spelt out their future dreams – Grafton wanted to write like Robert Lowell, Paul was going to South America to paint.

While the other boys sang and dreamed, Bill had been

content to cradle Grafton and stroke his hair. The boys
fell silent. Slowly Bill started speaking in a soft pure
voice:

> 'Wynken, Blynken and Nod one night
> Sailed off in a wooden shoe –
> Sailed on a river of crystal light
> Into a sea of dew.'

As he spoke the reflection of the stars became shoals of
herring fish, the gold of the moon sang of enchanted
lands. The other two took up Bill's refrain. As the
flagons emptied the questing boys cupped the ocean in
their hands, until the tide changed at dawn and they
returned to the jetty over the rocks in the morning of
Christmas Day.

> 'Now cast your nets wherever you wish –
> Never afeared are we;
> Cried the stars to the fishermen three:
> Wynken
> Blynken
> and Nod.'

So sang the bold, all-conquering boys to the beautiful
sea. Linked arm in arm, they walked back to shore
entirely without irony, jealousy or restraint.

How to Come Top

David ('Eggs') Ellery, my only friend in third form, had a huge head. He wore small round spectacles with wire frames, which barely covered his eyes. We sat together in the same desk at the back of the class and pulled each other off while Mr Selfrage, the freckled Latin Master, droned earnestly on. David insisted he worked at the Melbourne morgue every Christmas, but I didn't believe him. I always wanted to get it over quickly, but David preferred to take our time. He used to pull me off with his thumb and first finger joined in a donut. It took ages.

Two rows across from us, Barry Adams, the English form captain, and blond-haired Peter Feltham, who had almond-shaped eyes, pulled each other off as well. There, any similarity ended. Barry was always top of class and Peter extremely pretty, while David and I were regarded as of no account. In the row between us, tall Lance Farnett, looking like an underfed goose, sat enviously in a desk on his own. Lance was a dunce.

In the last week of term David asked some of the class to his birthday party. He said he was going to leave school and become a clerk with the AMP.

As always, I turned up early – to make sure I had the right address. David lived in Alma Road, St Kilda. I had never been to a flat before. Wearing his school suit, my friend answered the door. Inside, the curtains and carpet were shabby; the light bulb on the high ceiling without shade. David's mother was a tired woman with sad grey eyes and a head like a nut. His father, a TPI pensioner, had a terrible cough. Mr was considerably shorter than Mrs Ellery. As his parents thanked me for coming, saying that the others should be here soon, David carefully put my present – a book – at the end of the long table covered with party hats and bon bons. I had lime cordial, while Mrs Ellery drank sherry and Mr Ellery chainsmoked. We waited for an hour but no-one came. David's Mum poured another glass of sherry; his father, all sags and wrinkles, shook his head. Mrs Ellery said it meant there'd be more for us but we didn't believe her. David stood at the door like an old man, stringy body, sparse brown hair.

At three, after hot saveloys and little pies, Mrs Ellery packed a basket of food wrapped in cellophane, and the four of us walked to Luna Park. Even on the dodgems David didn't say a word. We rode the roller coaster three times, and once (it was my first time) took the Big Dipper. David and I sat close, holding each other, behind David's Mum and Mr Ellery who smoked all the while. We had lots and lots of fairy floss. At five o'clock I explained I had to be home for tea. I shook David's hand and wished him all the best. Mrs Ellery said she hoped I'd see David again. They waved me goodbye from under the Funnyman's teeth.

I rode back on the East Brighton tram, sitting outside by the door. During tea, Dad – a lapsed Catholic who'd had a nervous breakdown just before I was born – told a joke about Ava Gardner being lost in town. She was found under a stair, Fred Astaire. They were making On The Beach then. It was the only joke I ever heard him tell.

The next day, when Mother and Dad were out, I stripped naked, sat on my haunches on the carpet in front of the living-room mirror and lit a Turf cigarette which I'd taken from the secret supply Mother kept in the musical jug. I took out the vacuum cleaner, unfastened the attachment. The hose of the Hoover just fitted over my cock, which I greased with vaseline. Then I turned on the machine, lifting the hose carefully on and off so that the suction didn't drain out my intestines,

25

looking at myself in the mirror all the while, inhaling deeply on my cigarette. When I came, finger up my arse, I felt real, and amazingly powerful. Hanging on the living-room wall the grandfather man, made out of a coconut which uncle Jack had brought back from Malaya, smiled down his stringy beard at me. After he recovered from the War, Jack – a heavy drinker – had become Moran and Cato's top commercial traveller. My favourite relative, he married late and fell out with Mother over grandma's will.

Feeling empty again, I glanced into the mirror to see if I looked okay. Finishing my cigarette I packed up the machine. I wondered how long it would take to clog up. Wondered whether Avis, my mother, would notice. And if she'd care. Mostly I wondered about David. Wondered if he felt as strange in his parents' flat, inside his massive head, as I did here – so alone and disconnected. I tidied up and, in my underpants, watched from our glassed-in back verandah. The pink cyclamens in their pots were always kept inside; outside a withered yellow chrysanthemum lay on the lawn my Dad had clipped the evening before.

I opened the louvres. Next door at the Rawlings sang the muffled radio that I heard through my bedroom window when day after day I'd stayed home sick from primary school. Mr Rawlings had to take off his shoes before he was allowed inside their house. He and Mrs Rawlings were always arguing. I went back to the musical jug and stole another cigarette. I wondered if Mother really smoked. Why is it such a lonely business?

One Sunday morning, just before Mum and Dad and I were to visit Auntie Al's, there was ring at the front door. Although it was boiling hot, David was dressed in his grey school suit. He gave me a book of poems as an early present for Christmas, which was also my birthday. The four of us drove to Auntie Al's at Preston. David and I stayed outside, in the back seat of our black Hillman Minx. David said how glad he was I came to his party. He fished out my cock and started pulling me off, hands moving like a Balinese dancer's. Then he slipped off his glasses and put my cock in his mouth. He sucked me off slowly, in a most professional way; it was almost as good as the vacuum cleaner. When I came in his mouth, I felt, again, amazing. He said I tasted nice. Although we took him all the way home to St Kilda, I last remember David with his school tie and suitcoat on, putting back his glasses.

The third form notes came out on the last day of school. Barry Adams wrote good things about everyone else in 3C, including stupid Lance Farnett. But about my friend and I he said: 'David Ellery and Grafton Everest are going to write a book next year: *Howe to Cum Topp*'. I never found out what David thought, but when I read that coming home on the 64 tram I made up my mind I'd show the bastards.

Three years later, just before we sat for Matric in the Exhibition Buildings, I read in the *Age* that David had died in the Alfred Hospital of an overdose of tablets. Pretty Peter Feltham killed himself four years later. He blew his brains out with a double-barrelled shotgun. Barry Adams, his English friend, did Law, went to Oxford, and is now a Queen's Counsel. I never came top, but I got quite close. Avis, alone and nearly blind, is still alive in Melbourne.

II

There was a young man from the West
Was depressed and depressed and depressed
  And depressed and depressed
  And depressed and depressed
And depressed and depressed and depressed.
       Lennie Lower

All About Anthrax

'Good morning. It's time for work,' sang the pre-recorded clock radio with built-in cassette. Grafton stirred, felt ill as always, looked at his watch, swallowed some distilled water and a handful of Vitamin B1 and reached for the telephone. It was the same old story: 'I can't come in today. I'm sick.' Grafton was always sick. People accepted that as the most fundamental fact about him. But getting off work again was quite a different matter. Then from out of the inspired recesses of his knowledge-box sounded a voice: 'I've got anthrax.' For once there was no reply. Anthrax was one disease Wanda the departmental secretary hadn't heard of anyone having, not even hypochondriacal Grafton. No smart-arsed reply flowed out of Wanda's ruby lips this most unusual morning. She even sounded concerned. Unconsciously an almost warm 'I hope you feel better' filtered through the black holes in the telephone. 'Thank you,' he graciously replied. Grafton felt very pleased with himself. He read his 'Just for Today' card, took some Multivite, masturbated, and went back to sleep. He dreamt of anthrax.

Grafton woke at noon. He felt strangely alive. A creature of habit, he went about his normal indolent day (telephoning, taking tablets, drinking plenty of liquids, eating greens), but he couldn't get anthrax out of his mind. What did he know about anthrax? He suspected it had something to do with sheep or cattle. Hadn't there been an outbreak recently? In Victoria? In truth he didn't know.

Grafton's tertiary training came into play. He reached for the *Concise Oxford Dictionary* Mother Everest had given him for his thirtieth birthday, along with the *Tractatus*. Its blue, red, green and purple cover was still unruffled on the shelves. He picked at its crisp pages gingerly. It had never dawned on Grafton before that dictionaries too had page numbers, but there on p. 49 of his virgin book, between 'an'thrac/ite' and 'anthropocentric', was anthrax. He marvelled at the word: *an'thrax, n. Malignant boil; splenic fever of sheep and cattle; malignant pustule caused in man by infection from animals so affected. (L.f. Kk, – carbuncle).*

So it was in sheep and cattle. And human beings could get it. Grafton felt gratified at that. But it didn't tell him much. Was it serious? More importantly, could he have it? So many questions, his head pounded with possibilities.

He walked almost briskly across the road to where Toni the Greek and Icarus the Butcher idly clustered. 'How are we this afternoon?' they chorused with a smile. 'Not very well,' he replied in an unusually cavalier manner. 'What do you know about anthrax?' 'I know nothing,' said Toni with a shrug of shoulder. 'There's a none in my shop, I can tell you that,' announced Icarus firmly. 'Nor in mine,' said Toni as an after-thought. Grafton trudged home, unenlightened and temporarily put down.

Where *do* people find things out? Grafton's unused mind ticked over, slotting slowly into place. Of course! With tentative tread he went to the Main University Library. Grafton hadn't been in a library since the morning he finished his PhD. Having vowed never to read another book, he had thus far stuck to his resolve. Grafton hated libraries: the air-conditioning made him feel enclosed and he couldn't smoke.

As he entered the library door he saw an Indian lady on the entrance desk. A sign said Readers Assistance Unit. That sounded like his cup of tea. He felt slightly foolish until he asked, 'Can you help me? I need to find out all about anthrax.' As the words came out he felt much better. He asked for a pencil and some paper; then he asked the way to the lavatory. Asking, especially asking for help, Grafton had discovered many years ago, was his greatest gift. Perhaps his only one. He delighted in asking for the way or for the time, even when he knew. He liked to see his helpers' eyes light up at the idea that they were actually being of use. As Grafton asked and questioned the Indian lady's eyes positively shone.

Soon they were chatting. 'And how are you today?' Grafton always took that question literally. Before they had got to the real business at hand, Grafton had told her about his backache, kidney trouble, prostatitis, and piles. They were all connected. In his experience illness brought human beings together. It had worked again.

The librarian brought him *Black's Medical Diction-ary*, 1963 edition. Rather odd he thought. University had taught him to regard with suspicion any book more than three years old. Grafton settled down at his desk. He felt very important.

Immediately he looked up the Index – his training had taught him all the tricks – which directed him to pp. 51–2. There he read 'Anthrax – (Greek for coal)'. A mistake, a contradiction already! His scholarly mind rushed to the word he had added to his impoverished vocabulary the very night before. Grafton's languid memory cells reproduced: *an'thracite, n. Non-bituminous variety of coal. Hence-itic, it'ous, a.a. (f. Gk. anthrakitis, a kind of coal or as prec. + ITE'*

He didn't understand all the symbols. But there was a connection. Perhaps carbuncle and coal were the same word in Ancient Greek? He read on, transcribing in his childish hand. Grafton always printed. He had never learned to write. In fact he had managed to pass through childhood without growing up or acquiring basic skills. *Anthrax is a very serious disease occurring in South American and Australian sheep and cattle* (he under-lined 'very serious disease', and 'Australian sheep and cattle'), *and in those who tend them or handle the skins and fleece, even long after removal of the latter from the animals. It has also broken out occasionally in epidemics among wool-sorters or cattle-tenders . . .*

Grafton wrote in red ink in the margin 'Tanners/ wool sorters. Check.'

The cause is a bacillus (B. anthracis) which grows in long chains and produces spores of great vitality. These spores retain their life for years in dried skins and fleeces; they are not destroyed by boiling, freezing, 5 per cent carbolic lotion, or, like many bacilli, by the gastric juice. The disease is communicated from a diseased animal to a crack in the skin, e.g. of a shepherd or butcher or when it occurs in busy commercial centres, from contact with skins or fleeces. Nowadays skins are handled wet, but if they are allowed to dry, so that dust laden with spores is inhaled by the worker, an internal form of the disease results. Instances have occurred of the disease being conveyed on shaving brushes made from bristles of diseased animals. He tucked that information away for later use.

Symptoms a) External Form – this is the 'malignant pustule.' He liked the sound and sickening imagery of that. *After innoculation of some small wound, a few hours or days elapse, and then a red, inflamed swelling appears, which grows larger till it covers half the face or the breadth of the arm, as the case may be. Upon its summit appears a bleb of pus* ('a bleb of pus' Grafton repeated to himself), *which bursts and leaves a black scab, perhaps half an inch wide. There is at the same time great prostration and fever. The inflammation may last ten days or so, when it slowly subsides and the patient recovers, if surviving the fever and prostration.*

Grafton was fascinated. It all seemed magical, and much more interesting than rabies, or any of the diseases he had known.

b) Internal Form – This takes the form of pneumonia with haemorrhages, when the spores have been drawn into the lungs or of ulcers of the stomach and intestines, with gangrene of the spleen, when they (the spores) have

34

been swallowed. ('Inhaled or Ingested' Grafton wrote in red). *It is usually fatal in two or three days.*

'IT IS USUALLY FATAL IN TWO OR THREE DAYS.' Grafton felt his heart beat, and marked this with an asterisk. He had to go outside, for air. He lit up a cigarette, his first in fifteen days. The Seventh Day Adventists couldn't save him now.

The hero noted on.

Treatment. Prevention is most important by disinfecting with superheated steam all contaminated fleeces, and all fleeces coming from a district where the sheep have anthrax. All hides should be handled wet, so that spores cannot be present in dust, for the internal form is four times as fatal as the external. On this little known fact Grafton's eyes focused and refocused. He readily absorbed that hands of workmen must be carefully washed before eating, and working clothes changed. Even though Mother Everest had made him scrupulous, Grafton decided to wash more often and change his clothes twice daily. *By these means the number of deaths from anthrax, in the English woollen manufacturing districts, has been reduced to a tenth of the number that occurred fifty years ago.*

Grafton finished the fullstop with a flourish and printed very neatly, 'Black's Medical Dictionary 1963 edit. pp. 51–2'.

He reached for Book No. 2. The opening information was very much the same:

Anthrax is an acute infectious disease caused by Bacillus anthracis (to Grafton it already seemed like a friend) *principally involving herbivorous animals from which it is transferred to man. Two forms of human anthrax exist: the external form affecting the skin and subcutaneous tissue and the internal form resembling pneumonia, meningitis and intestinal infections.*

Warming to his task Grafton ploughed on:

Man contracts the disease principally from handling infected animal carcasses, hides, hair, wool, brushes, bone-meal, and other animal by-products. Hangnails and skin injuries in workers handling animals and their by-products predispose to infection.

The term 'anthrax' is derived from the Greek 'anthrakos' meaning coal ('So that settles that!', he wrote in brackets) *and refers to the black eschar* (sore) *typical of cutaneous anthrax. The malignant pustule is a* <u>*little papule*</u> (Grafton gratuitously underlined) *which blisters, ulcerates, sloughs and develops around it a brownish swelling; constitutional disturbance may be severe.*

Grafton digested the fact that fleas, ticks, and other insects may transmit the infection from animal to animal or from animal to man. Thumbing the diverse books and articles on the desk, he learnt of the perils of handling infected bones. Never work in a glue factory. He was fascinated by the case of a man who got anthrax after pruning roses. One daily newspaper wanted to write a story of how anthrax bacilli could rise from the ground in the sap of a rose, but it turned cut that the man kept his secateurs on a shelf in his garden shed next to a bag of contaminated bone-meal.

After the 'cases' Grafton came to some Horrid Photographs.

Fig. 1. ANTHRAX of neck with secondary lesions on chest.
Fig. 2. Same patient: oedema spreading to scrotum. (The sad look on the man's face, Grafton decided, corresponded exactly to a person with oedema spreading to the scrotum!!)

Grafton felt in his element. He hadn't been so interested for years. As he scavenged the pages, he was amazed to find all sorts of anthrax.

Cerebral anthrax – from invasion of the brain by bacilli headed the list. (Grafton's mind boggled as he wrote in red.) After Intestinal anthrax, Malignant anthrax, anthrax septicaemia and Skin anthrax he spied *Pulmonary anthrax or Wool-sorters' disease* – caused by circulating bacilli which produces a severe pneumonia. This especially took his fancy.

More and more he focused on fatal inhalation anthrax. Grafton was asthmatic – he knew the dangers of breathing, and breathing in. 'Severe, fatal pulmonary infections result from inhalation of anthrax spores,' he wrote, avidly instancing the case of a man who worked in a shop adjacent to a goat-hair processing mill. 'They're deathly even from a distance,' he repeated to himself.

Grafton learnt that cutaneous cases can be cured by antibiotics; the inhalatory type, though very rare, are almost always *fatal*. Latest figures show forty-five cases of pulmonary anthrax reported in England, USA and Australia in the last hundred years. *Forty-one out of the forty-five cases were fatal*. Grafton realised he'd hit upon an important fact. *Pulmonary Anthrax* – he savoured the words, closed his book, and walked out of the Main Library with a satisfied smile.

He went to a milk bar and throwing caution to the wind ordered a strawberry malted milk shake and a doubleheaded chocolate icecream. Deciding to keep a file he bought a manilla folder. He wrote proudly on the outside 'All About Anthrax', G. Everest. If lost return to sender.'

On the way home Grafton called in at the butchers.

'A pound of pork chops,' he said pleasantly.

'None left,' answered Icarus without looking up.

'What ya mean you've got no pork chops,' replied Grafton menacingly as he reached over the counter, Icarus's cleaver in his hand. Frustration of desire was one thing Grafton didn't accept with equanimity.

Simmering down, he accepted a leg of lamb.

'Do you realize that anthrax spores can remain alive in dry earth for over sixty years?' offered Grafton as a gesture of conciliation.

As a matter of fact Icarus didn't. He continued sweeping up the sawdust and contemplated the absurdity of the human predicament.

'Did you know that the golden rule in medicine should be that any worker in a tannery or a bone-meal factory with a septic pimple has anthrax unless proved otherwise?' continued Grafton unperturbed.

'You're insane,' announced Icarus.

'Do you realize that this carcass could be riddled with anthrax?' cried Grafton, twirling the joint above his head. 'Worse, that hordes of anthrax spores could be hovering around this very room?'

'Go take a flying fuck,' retorted Icarus, turning off the light. Too much education, he realized, was indeed a dangerous thing. His old mother in Crete had been right.

'Pulmonary anthrax is Death,' screamed Grafton as Icarus pelted him out of the shop.

Grafton crossed the road and planted his foot into Merlin the doberman pinscher who wagged the place where his tail used to be. He kicked the dog again and headed for the Gallipoli Delicatessen.

'You look fine,' said Toni, passing over a pint of milk as Grafton's sixteen stone lumbered in. Instead Grafton took some barley sugar.

'Pasteurization can't cure anthrax. The spores lie dormant, they lie moribund in the ground. M.O.R.I.B.U.N.D.,' spelled Grafton with Toni's pen, half aware it wasn't quite the right word. Grafton prided himself on being an educator of unfortunates.

'Anthrax was the first disease for which the causative organism was isolated.' Toni was far away. 'Pasteur discovered it . . . and Robert Koch.' Toni's eyes brightened. He knew all about cock. 'Pasteur and Koch. And they couldn't cure it,' said Grafton regretting his previous milk shake.

'Elephants get anthrax, did ya know that?' Toni shook his head.

'Four Nigerian vets contracted anthrax from conducting a post-mortem on an infected elephant. A piano-key maker got it from the ivory keys made of elephant tusks. And a sculptress died from anthrax after carving statuettes from horse bones.'

Toni the Greek knew all Anglo Saxons were crazy!

*   *   *

38

Grafton picked up some Disprin and headed home to a fridge full of applejuice and mackerel. He had joined Weight Watchers the week before. Grafton wondered about fish.

The next morning there was a knock at the door. It was Kitty – the Japanese Seventh Day Adventist. She had been his 'buddy' the last time he had attended the Five-Day Stop Smoking Plan. Grafton had been five times to the Five-Day Plan. The fifth time he lasted a day.

'Have you been smoking?' asked Kitty in her social worker voice.

'I broke again today,' answered Grafton guiltily. 'When I get nervous or excited I have to have something in my mouth.'

'So do I,' she said demurely eyeing his dormant member and stepping out of her kimono.

Grafton realized something was up. Kitty was kneeling down mouthing his cock. 'I'm glad you came,' said Grafton carefully taking off his clothes. He left his singlet on. While she tongued him, he languidly munched her cunty centre. Soon he became enthusiastic. Spreading Kitty's thighs, he hungrily nosed her erectile tissue.

'Take me,' moaned Kitty in a desperate voice. Splaying her buttocks wide, a pudgy hand on each cheek, he threaded her outer rim.

'Tell me all you know about anthrax,' commanded Grafton in his punishing voice.

'Ohh . . . in sheep,' she gasped in an orbit of come.

'I know that already,' he said thrustingly.

'Cows, goats . . . More,' she pleaded. Her tight arse moved in a fiery rhythm to meet and circle his throbbing cock. Kitty hadn't been sodomised before on a mission of mercy. She was thoroughly enjoying herself.

'Pigs. In pigs,' she squealed as Grafton plunged in deep.

'Pigs?' he said thoughtfully, and withdrew.

'Do they really?' he said to the pleasured Japanese. 'I don't believe you.

39

'Pigs eat babies, do you know that?' said a pensive Grafton. 'If they get a taste for baby blood they want nothing else.' As he spoke he realized his mistake. 'Pigs do get it, especially hamsters. And eagles. Did you know that Bacilli anthracis has been isolated in the faeces of eagles?

'Elephants too,' he added, recalling the case of the four Nigerian vets. 'No one's safe.'

'That was the best fuck I ever had,' said the smoking Kitty. 'Please don't smoke, just for today. Otherwise my coming won't have been worthwhile,' she said with an inscrutable smile.

'I've got a joke,' said Grafton, adjusting his singlet until it covered his back. 'The answer is "Chicken Sukiyaki". What is the question?'

'Fuck me again,' begged Kitty. 'In the cunt. Please.'

'The question my dear Kitty is "Who is the oldest living Kamikaze pilot?" '

'Chicken Sukiyaki,' roared Grafton holding his sides. 'Get it?'

'He was my father,' said Kitty sadly putting on her kimono, and lighting up.

Kitty Sukiyaki, Seventh Day Adventist, left in tears.

'It's a hard life if you don't weaken,' philosophized Grafton from the door. 'That's life,' he said gratuitously and grilled some fish for lunch.

The next day was Tuesday. Grafton went to see his physician every Tuesday.

'Good afternoon, Doctor,' said Dr Bryan O'Brien.

'Good afternoon, Doctor,' retorted Grafton with a smile. Old friends, they loved playing this game. Grafton had a PhD in political science. Dr O'Brien constantly endeared himself by pointing out that Grafton was a Real Doctor.

'You look fine. What's the matter today?' quipped Bryan O'Brien as he gave Grafton his regular weekly anal massage. Grafton rose prostatically from his chair; the treatment still hadn't done the trick.

Dr O'Brien was a Catholic cupboard drinker with twinkling eyes. He was a wife beater who fancied himself as a spy.

'You're taking far too many vitamins,' said Bryan O'Brien removing his glove and washing his fingers.

'Here's something that might interest you. A group of boy scouts in Oregon went hiking in the Rocky Mountains and killed a grizzly bear. They roasted the bear and ate its liver. And all fourteen boy scouts died of an overdose. Of Vitamin D poisoning! The moral of that story is don't eat grizzly bear's liver and don't take too many vitamin pills.'

Grafton was silent.

'What is the matter today?' said Bryan O'Brien.

'What do you know about anthrax?' asked Grafton.

'Anthrax!' said Dr O'Brien. He did remember one case of a tanner when he was a Junior Resident at St Cecilia's.

'Ghastly disease – awful black sores.' A smile flickered across Bryan O'Brien's face. 'The same day I treated a nun with the clap. She got it from a lay teacher . . . Like that?' he sniggered.

Grafton ignored the other very infectious disease. 'But that'd be external anthrax – from a cut in the skin. Ninety-eight per cent of human anthrax is of the cutaneous type. The man didn't die, did he?' said Grafton, amazing his physician with his medical expertise.

'What do you know about pulmonary anthrax – from breathing in spores? I'm interested in extermination,' added Grafton.

Bryan O'Brien's face darkened.

'I'll only do away with Leftists, and Welfare Statists,' Grafton reassured him.

Bryan O'Brien peeped outside. Two patients remained in the waiting room. He told them to come back another day. With Medicare it didn't matter how few you got through. Most of his patients now were imaginary.

'After you, Doctor,' said Dr O'Brien closing the surgery. At the doctor's opulent Rose Bay home Grafton outlined his queries.

'How could you kill people (how many people?) with pulmonary anthrax? What would be the most effective method? Would you be likely to be discovered? How unlikely?' The questions ran like water.

Bryan O'Brien found plotting death much more invigorating than healing the sick and helping the infirm and lame. Over vodka and orange juice (the vodka for Bryan, the juice for Grafton) they formulated their plan.

'Psittacosis,' shrieked Dr O'Brien's parrot while murder was being hatched.

As Bryan O'Brien talked, looking out to sea, dreaming of painless divorce and a pure form of free enterprise, Grafton printed on a prescription pad in his clumsy hand:

PLAN
Isolate and cultivate a very virulent strain of Bacillus Anthracis (not very difficult to do).
Make a broth culture of the bacillus.

'Bacteria exposed to oxygen give off spores and in turn spores produce bacteria. Right?' said Grafton. 'Right on,' answered Dr O'Brien.

Use a CIG machine to give you an aerosol of concentrated anthrax spores.
Then feed spores through air-conditioning into closed room.

'The combination of unusually large numbers of spores and a highly virulent strain will produce a massive infecting dose,' announced Bryan O'Brien sagely, pouring himself another neat vodka and tossing popcorn to the parrot.

Grafton thought he'd get a job as a janitor to gain access to the air-conditioning system of an important building; better still he'd pretend to be a janitor or a plumber for the brief period required. Unnecessary work was burdensome.

'But there's a catch,' said Bryan O'Brien. 'If twenty people were in the room we'd be unlikely to knock off the lot. It's an unfortunate fact that there are very few fatal illnesses that kill everybody affected, even pulmonary anthrax.'

'That's a shame,' said Grafton. 'What about three?' It was his lucky number.

Bryan O'Brien offered a better move:

B) *Better move*
Cultivate very virulent highly resistant strain.
Make broth culture.
Produce high dose, oily suspension of anthrax culture while victim asleep or drugged.
Because, when asleep, basic protective breathing mechanism doesn't work.

'Why not?' entreated Grafton.

'Because,' answered the doctor testily. 'This method would be certain to score three out of three,' he said, ignoring Grafton's query.

'How certain?' Grafton pressed.

'Life's uncertain,' philosophized Bryan O'Brien. 'But you take it from me, all three would be dead as a dinner.'

'If they were three unrelated cases, and especially if done in winter, there's little chance of an autopsy. And even if there were a post mortem, doctors at least in the city are unlikely to think of anthrax.'

'How unlikely?'

'Very.'

'It may surprise you to know that few physicians know much about anthrax,' said Bryan O'Brien. 'Death by severe viral influenza or pneumonia would almost certainly be the finding.'

'Country practitioners might pick it up if they thought of the possibility,' he added apologetically. 'But we'd feed the victims such a massive dose that they couldn't be saved,' pronounced the doctor with a smile.

Returning from the sideboard he pulled a text from the shelf. '*The clinical diagnosis of pulmonary anthrax* rests largely on knowledge of the patient's occupation and the exclusion of other causes of sudden prostrating illness with signs of pulmonary oedema or haemoptysis . . . So you're safe as houses.'

'All very macabre,' Grafton thought gleefully. But he still preferred the air-conditioning method.

'Psittacosis,' repeated parrot O'Brien, munching a matzo ball. It was the only word he knew.

Bryan O'Brien gave him some numbers to ring – immunologists, the School of Public Health and the Department of Tropical Medicine, the Professor of Chest Medicine, and an old friend specializing in infectious diseases at the Blue Light Clinic.

'Tell me how you go,' said Bryan O'Brien showing him to the door. 'And cut down on those vitamins . . . they're deadly.'

Grafton went home, poured some distilled water, took his prostatitis pills, reflected on the marvels of modern medicine and reached for the telephone.

'Hello, Dr Everest here.'

'Hello Doctor,' reciprocated Professor Porton-Lamb of the Department of Tropical Medicine. 'Can I help?'

'You can indeed,' Grafton responded earnestly. 'Could you tell me how many cases of pulmonary anthrax there's been in the last ten years?'

'None I'm pleased to say,' replied the puzzled Professor.

'But it'd be very hard to diagnose, wouldn't it?' questioned Grafton.

'What exactly do you mean by that?' said Porton-Lamb.

'Well,' said Grafton, 'if one made an aerosol of anthrax bacilli and fed it through the air-conditioning, everyone in the room who died would almost certainly be certified as dying of viral pneumonia.' (You should be certified thought Professor Porton-Lamb.) 'Unless they thought of anthrax,' continued Grafton, 'and doctors in the city wouldn't, would they?'

For the first time in his long and uneventful career, Professor Porton-Lamb could hear the authentic voice of a psychopath.

'That is an interesting proposition,' humoured the good professor. 'I suppose you're right.'

'Do you mind if I come over and have a chat,' Grafton asked warmly.

'Mother Mary save me,' mumbled the man of science, 'I'm off to a symposium ... today ... in Uganda,' faltered his rabbit voice. 'I suggest you consult the Annual Report of the Director General,' he said, pulling himself together and using his professorial voice. 'Why don't you research the matter yourself? ... And do send me the results,' said Porton-Lamb hanging up.

His head swimming with ideas and encouraged by other calls, G. Everest, Academic, set to do some more Research.

Grafton knew he now needed more specialized knowledge than the General Library could provide, so he headed for the Bio-Med Library at the other end of campus.

Eagerly he rummaged through the index cards, but to no avail.

'Do you realize there is no entry under anthrax?' Grafton thundered at the attendant, a de-tribalized Lebanese by the look of him.

Apologetically, the attendant slithered around the room, plucking books and journal articles from the shelves. 'This should help,' he whimpered, giving a bundle to Grafton and showing him to a very large desk.

There were all sorts of books about anthrax. Plus anthrax exotica like '17 Cases of Human Anthrax in the Upper Volta' and 'The History of Anthrax in Moldavia'. Grafton passed over 'Anthrax – a health hazard at the bottom of the garden?' and 'Human Anthrax in Iran – Report of 33 cases and review of literature' and, pencil in claw, started first on 'An Epidemic of Inhalation Anthrax: The First in the Twentieth Century' by

Brachman, Plotkin, Bumford and Atchison.[1] Grafton read of a sudden outbreak of inhalation anthrax in a New Hampshire goat-hair processing mill. Because of the combination of unusually large numbers of spores and highly virulent strain, five pulmonary cases occurred. Again four out of five were fatal. Everything was fitting into place.

Grafton's beady eyes settled next on 'The clinical aspects of anthrax' by A.B. Christie, MA, MD, FRCP, FFCM, DPH: *Post-graduate Medical Journal* (August 1973) **49**, 565–570. Unerringly he headed for the Summary: *The incidence of pulmonary anthrax is related to the number and size of anthrax-containing particles which are inhaled. Artificial mists containing lethal doses of anthrax bacilli can be manufactured.* 'Perfect!' wrote Grafton in the margin in red. Bryan O'Brien was no mug after all. This was Grafton's highest form of praise.

Soon Grafton came to a strange mixture of science and theology – so typical of the Academy's higher reaches.

In the 9th chapter of Exodus the Lord instructed Moses to demand from Pharaoh the release of the Israelites on pain of a grievous murrain ('Note the internal rhyme!' Grafton wrote mischievously on the pad) *to descend exclusively on the cattle of Egypt. Pharaoh was unmoved and his cattle died. The Lord again instructed Moses and Aaron to take a handful of ashes and sprinkle it towards heaven in the sight of Pharaoh. There occurred a boil breaking forth with blanes upon man and beast throughout all the land of Egypt. There can be little doubt that this is one of the earliest accounts of an outbreak of anthrax, and the handful of ashes must have been transformed into an aerosol of bacilli. Virgil described the illness no less vividly in the third book of the Georgics, where all the*

1. *Philip S. Brachman, Stanley A. Plotkin, Forrest H. Bumford and Mary M. Atchison:* 'An epidemic of Inhalation Anthrax: The First in the Twentieth Century', *American Journal of Hygiene,* Vol. 72, No. 1, July 1960, pp. 6–23.

symptoms and signs of the disease as it attacks beasts in the fields or in the stalls are set forth, often with surprisingly modern epidemiological detail.

A.B. Christie, MA, MD, FRCP, FFCM, DPH, DCH, from Fazakerly Hospital, Liverpool, was indeed a literate man!

For relief, Grafton leafed through two investigations on the lethal effect of anthrax aerosols before returning to Christie again. Grafton thought the name was entirely appropriate to the matter at hand.

Christie was back to the Bible analoguing Exodus and the idea of bacteriological warfare: *The organism and its spores can be produced in almost unlimited amounts in the laboratory and much experimental work has been done on the aerosol dispersion of the spores. Virulent antibiotic resistant strains have been produced in the laboratory through selection procedures. Macfarlane Burnet and David White in the fourth edition of their book* Natural History of Infectious Diseases, *C.U.P., 1972 in a chapter headed 'Perils and Possibilities' make this statement: 'It is physically possible to produce in a room a thin mist of bacteria so that any animal that takes a few breaths in that room will die, unless it is subsequently treated with an appropriate drug. To produce similar conditions over the large volume of air within and around an enemy city is physically possible, and in all probability the technical methods of achieving this have already been perfected. A ton of anthrax spores would contain about 10^{18} individual spores. If these could be uniformly distributed in a volume of air six or seven miles across and extending 300 feet upwards from the ground, each litre of air (about one deep breath) would contain about 100,000 spores.'*

They do not suggest that such uniform distribution could be achieved, but they do suggest that 'the number of bacteria that could be carried in a single plane or in a single cluster of bombs might produce a startlingly large toll of illness and death.' The numbers are certainly far higher than those used in Brachman's monkey experiments or counted in his goat hair mill.

Grafton learnt that heavy concentrations of anthrax

spores sprayed in the air could result in up to 70–80 per cent fatalities in untreated cases; vaccines available at present might not avail against aerosol exposure. Decontamination of food and the environment and restocking with livestock would be rendered difficult for a long period. *Air carriage of spores would contaminate localities far distant from the area of immediate attack. Anthrax would persist for long periods in a resistant spore form which could be spread over very large distances by wind carriage in the course of time.*

'So it's all taken on a different complexion now!' he printed in his shaky hand.

Grafton sensed he'd stumbled onto something *very significant*. Christie's article went on to talk about intestinal anthrax in South West Africa, but Grafton was too stunned to read any further. Like Bryan O'Brien, he had always thought of himself as a spy and rather fancied the idea of knocking off a few renegade socialists, but bacteriological warfare – exterminating whole populations, wiping out cities – was too much altogether. He packed his books, swallowed some Buscopan and Brufen, picked up his umbrella, lit up a cigarette and walked out into the rain. His arthritis had suddenly come back again and the wet made it worse.

Everything had got out of hand. He wished he'd never heard of anthrax.

Grafton needed time to think. What better place than a hospital? Apart from the confusion the new information engendered, he was worried about his prick. It was dribbling again.

The thought of his admission cheered him up. Grafton never felt so well, so alive as when he was going into hospital. It was a familiar place and the food was good. He'd had eight admissions to St Cecilia's Private.

This time he was in for a cystoscopy. Grafton pulled his Doctor's rank and wouldn't let the orderly shave his pubic hairs. They got itchy and took so long to grow.

The pre-med made every operation worthwhile.

Grafton closed his eyes waiting for the Omnipon to work. Soon he was away in the land of cosmic visions and powerful vibrations. Under the anaesthetic Grafton babbled, 'I've got it – anthrax.'

'No you haven't,' said the surgeon reassuringly.

'Rabies more likely,' the doctor confided to the winking nurse.

'Anthrax,' Grafton groaned. Soon they were probing his prick. They found nothing of interest there.

Grafton went straight from hospital to the STD Clinic. He'd been there many times with NSU. Recently he'd picked up a strain of Mozambique Rose.

Dr Stet-Lupin from Athens, Georgia, was a thin man with hawk nose, dandruff and burnt-out eyes. He wore a starched white coat with a red poppy pinned to the lapel. The antiseptic interior of the STD Clinic counterpointed its blue-stone walls.

'What do you know about anthrax and bacteriological warfare?' asked Grafton exposing his prick.

'How did you get onto me?' Dr Stet-Lupin asked slyly.

'Bryan O'Brien told me to make contact.'

'Well he shouldn't have,' drawled the Director petulantly.

Calming down, Stet-Lupin admitted that he was an authority; as a matter of fact he'd written a number of articles. 'Classified, of course.'

Reaching in his drawer, amongst closeted condoms, ointments and pessaries, Dr Stet-Lupin read aloud:

'*Micro-organisms of epidemic infectious diseases may be deliberately disseminated as a weapon of war*'.

'It is no secret that the major powers have been carrying out research on bacterial warfare,' confided Dr Stet-Lupin.

'*There are many possibilities for manipulating currently circulating strains of micro-organisms for warfare purposes, by producing antigenically modified or antibiotic-resistant types that would by-pass available prophylactic or therapeutic procedures*,' he read with pride.

'There are obvious technical difficulties in producing and utilizing bacteria in war, but given enough time and money these difficulties can be overcome. The only hope is that hand in hand with research on how to use bacteria in war, paralled research must be carried out on the ways of protecting one's own troops against what could be a double-edged weapon'.

Stet-Lupin listed the prime biological agents in warfare with the gusto and dedication of a compulsive gambler reciting the form. He spoke in a shrill, chilled voice:

'Viruses, such as those causing influenza, yellow fever, Eastern equine encephalitis and psittacosis.' Grafton remembered parrot O'Brien.

'Rickettsiae, such as those causing epidemic typhus, Q fever and Rocky Mountain spotted fever.' The Rockies must be very dangerous thought Grafton, recalling the Boy Scouts. Bryan O'Brien loomed back into mind.

'Bacteria, such as those causing typhoid fever and cholera or which produce tularaemia, brucellosis, the plague, and of course Anthrax.'

'There's Fungi and Toxins too.

'Anthrax is the most deadly. But personally I prefer plague. Pneumonic plague. I've got a deep sense of history.'

Grafton was thunderstruck.

'When you're dealing with ruthless people you have to use ruthless methods,' announced Dr Stet-Lupin. 'They do. It's us or them.'

'I suppose you do,' said Grafton, wondering who 'they' were and whether Stet-Lupin used the same philosophy in his treatment of venereal disease.

'Most governments prefer either pneumonic plague or anthrax. As a matter of fact the British government dropped scatter bombs of very resistant anthrax spores on an island off the Scottish coast. It's now out of bounds.'

'Where can I find out about it?' asked Grafton.

'There was a film, but the authorities burnt it,' said Stet-Lupin sadly.

'Why don't you go and see the Department of Army? On second thoughts they wouldn't see you. Why don't you use Medlars – the computerised information retrieval system?

'Sorry I can't be more help. But there is some good news. Your blood test has just come back and you're clear as a whistle again.

'One thing. Don't mention my name,' said Dr Stet-Lupin. 'Please remember that.'

After discounting the Department of Army, Grafton took up the Director's suggestion that he use the Information Retrieval System of Index Medicus.

Grafton went back to the Bio-Med Library, and submitted a search request.

His entry read:

'Anthrax – Bacteriological Warfare

'Pulmonary Anthrax – Incidence, Diagnosis, Prevention, Research'

'I think you'll need a clearance for this,' said the distressed librarian.

'I'm a Doctor. I've a right to know,' snarled Grafton in his standover voice as the request was fed into the central Medlars computer in Canberra.

At headquarters bells rang, the warning buzzer sounded. In its all-embracing, value-neutral wisdom, Computer Sigma Zero determined that some clown had stumbled onto something he shouldn't have. The computer produced a print-out: 'This Information is Highly Classified. REPEAT. This Information is Highly Classified. Send agent to see person programming. REPEAT. Send agent.'

High-level machinery started moving. Grafton had tripped the switch.

Although he remained blissfully unaware, Grafton was caught in a real web of intrigue.

At home Grafton was exhausted. The front bell rang.

With all the energy of a fat dog Grafton stumbled to the door. As he nudged it open, a young woman with

51

lascivious brown eyes and a boyish face, wearing school uniform, her hair in pigtails, came into view. She carried a basket under one arm, and held a Pifco vibrator under the other like a baton.

'Hello, I'm Mercedes Underwood – the girl from EXT. You're the man who wanted to know about anthrax?'

Grafton nodded.

'I've brought you some strawberries and cream to eat,' she said sweetly, taking off her panties and lavishly spreading a large helping over her cunt.

Even though he had just eaten, Grafton did feel hungry. He munched happily at home in Strawberry fields.

Grafton looked up, frothing.

'You look undernourished,' he said reaching for a jar of Giant Economy Size Vegemite and anointing his pride with the tacky, black substance.

'It's full of Vitamin B1 – that'll bring your appetite back,' said Grafton nosing eagerly back to the strawberries.

'You are a clown,' Mercedes said sucking hungrily and coming up for air, 'wanting to know all about anthrax.'

Soon Grafton reached for the baby oil. As he turned her over he saw 'Mercedespops. Please use this side up' etched in indelible ink on her arse. Indeed I shall, he assented.

Why did he always sodomize women, Grafton mused. He didn't want to hurt them or him. But he strongly felt, despite the immediate pleasure, that he would be punished terribly.

Although Avis never told him so directly, Grafton knew that it was wrong, wrong, wrong. In fact whenever he did it he thought of Avis. She wasn't smiling. Yet he also knew it made him strong.

Treading her like a hen, Grafton could see his glistening cock, veins protruberant, thrusting in and out. Grafton honed in on the crimson amethyst. He pressed the vibrator to her cunt again.

'That's driving me crazy. I can't stand it,' she yelped.

Mercedes' clitoris was very tender. Grafton realized she'd have to have her mind taken off the sensitivity.

He hit upon an idea. 'Let's sing a hymn.'

'Onward Christian soldiers, marching *off to war*,' moaned Mercedes while he vibrated her cunt and continued sodomizing. Grafton arched her back and plunged in his wand right up to the hilt of her centre of hurt. Grafton felt like the cock of the walk.

'Je-zus, I'm coming. I'm coming,' shrieked Mercedes, clawing the air.

Grafton was feasting with panthers. He had never felt so powerful.

'How long have I been here?' he moaned. He felt like the dreaded tsetse fly had bitten him.

As he came out of the coma Grafton realized he was in a net and he couldn't get out. A young lamb lay down beside him.

He awoke to see The Group wearing gas masks (grey, deathly, eyes like glass, nozzles swinging) dancing a dance of death around him: elegant and circular.

Among swirling figures Grafton could decipher Icarus, the Indian lady, Mercedes still in pigtails, 'Why were they here?' he gasped.

Looking up he saw multi-coloured spores flowing through the air-conditioning.

Grafton felt sick and chilled. He started to vomit and cough up blood. In high temperature he had sensations of falling. Suspended. As in a labyrinth of air. His chest was full of moist sounds, heart rapid, his pulse feeble. Sweating profusely, he had never been so frightened.

Dr O'Brien, the parrot on his shoulder, was playing the harpsichord. The Lebanese librarian beat a drum.

'The Gulf of Benin,' Wanda the Secretary sang. 'Few came out, but many went in.' The dancers danced about him, shrieking. The circle kept closing in.

Grafton's head was pounding. Fire rained on Dresden. Scatter-bombs were falling.

Grafton knew he was trapped. He tried to get out but

the net tightened. The lamb whimpered, nudging his breast.

The dancing circle opened like an orchid and Kitty Sukiyaki appeared clad in khaki costume.

Hatred in her heart, the weapon of vengeance on her hip, she machine-gunned the lamb.

'God grant me the serenity to accept the things I cannot change,' Grafton mumbled like a mantra. He was splattered in the blood of the lamb.

'There's the man who wanted to know all about anthrax,' chorused the Circle.

'Too much knowledge is indeed a dangerous thing,' said Icarus, eating bread from the space where his face should have been.

'So that's the cosmic pay-back,' thought Grafton, inhaling weakly.

He shuddered and coughed up more blood.

A black bat hovered, talons tearing. Alsatian dogs with fangs bared snarled and menaced. The ceiling came crashing down. Animals lay dazed and dying. The multi-coloured spores continued to flow.

Grafton had always been amazed at the reality of other people's lives. The ultimate reality was closing in.

For three days and nights the circle throbbed around him. Bryan O'Brien felt his pulse and drank more wine. 'Take what you want from the universe, but pay.' Dr Stet-Lupin placed his poppy on Grafton's chest. The man who knew all about anthrax was dead.

'I know nothing,' said Toni setting fire to the room.

The King of Croatia

'Welcome to Gethsemene,' said the Gardener directing Grafton to the Enquiry Counter. Dressed in a suit, Grafton carried a half-open box of Black Magic and a withered rose. He proffered a soft chocolate but the Gardener refused. 'Blessed are they which hunger after righteousness for they shall be filled.' The Gardener spoke in a high-pitched foreign tone that was difficult to understand unless one listened intently. Grafton seldom did. However he did take heed of Mother who had asked him to visit Grandfather in the twilight home. There was money involved.

Grandfather Everest sat motionless under the Holy Mary. He was one of forty old men sitting in a perfectly straight line against the verandah wall. The opposite wall was glassed-in and the residents of the Old Men's Home looked out on another ward verandah, exactly the same as their own. It was Saturday but no one knew. There were no clocks, no calendars. Only the crucifix, and rows of the Virgin Mary, Mother of God. Deafening mood music was piped through the walls. While the other inmates engaged in occupational therapy – assembling useless articles – Grandfather Everest sat hunched over in his straight-backed chair, gazing steadily at the floor. He did not alter position as the sisters passed without speaking back and forth in front of him.

In a room of his own, an old man sat drinking what looked like warm milk. His face was swollen like a starfish. He was playing with a doll made out of his blond and boyish hair. A glistening white flower stood erect on the mantelpiece. The room streamed with light.

'Tomoslav's crazy,' said Matron Mores, as she marched Grafton past the room. 'He thinks he's the King of Croatia!'

'Old people are so ugly!' she pronounced with distaste, 'and totally unaware . . . No one ever comes to see him – poor old thing,' she said, pointing to Grandfather Everest on the verandah.

'Hello Poppa,' said Grafton, trying to conjure up some family resemblance in the incontinent old man.

Grandfather Everest answered in a soft, slurred voice, 'The lonely, lovely dead,' and cried.

A beautiful woman, tall and blond, wearing size-12 shoes and dressed in white, was checking the old man's pulse, oblivious to the odour and spreading stain. The Matron genuflected behind her. Grafton was entranced.

'Dr Everest, this is Dr Old. Dr Old, this is Dr Everest,' said Matron Mores, who rearranged the rubber sheet and left.

'Please call me Grafton,' said Grafton, noticing no ring of gold on the fourth finger of the physican's slender hand.

'Please call me Cynthia,' said Dr Old lifting her unmarried eyes.

Cynthia Old, right hand outstretched and poised, asked 'How do you do?' Grafton always took that question literally.

'Not very well I'm afraid. My nose is blocked, my bowels are loose and I've lost my equilibrium. I've got a terrible temperature . . .' On and on his symptomatology gushed while Grandfather Everest dribbled and leaked beside him.

'My arthritis and asthma are killing me, my piles are protruding and I just can't stop smoking.'

Cynthia was fascinated. Here was a healthy, robust young man talking endlessly of illness. He sounded like the man of her dreams.

'How do I look?' said Grafton, mournfully gazing into the physician's grey-green eyes.

56

'Fine, just fine,' said Cynthia Old, thrusting a thermometer deep down Grandfather Everest's frail arc of mouth.

With a vast exercise of will Grafton pulled himself out of his hypochondriacal self-obsession.

'What is a beautiful young woman like you doing in a place like this?' asked Grafton as an opener.

'I specialize in psychogeriatric problems,' replied Cynthia in a soothing, sensual voice. 'In fact I'm the editor of *The Australian and New Zealand Journal of Geriatric Psychiatry* and acting vice-president of the Australian Association of Gerontologists.' Cynthia's dedication made Grafton melt with admiration. 'But why . . .?'

'When one's been called "Old" from the first moment of birth one develops an interest in the process of aging,' she replied with an understanding smile.

So here was a woman actually trained to look after the infirm, the mad and the lame. Here was a woman whose chosen calling was looking after the sick . . . for ever! Grafton's heart pounded. He had to marry Cynthia Old. Before he was permanently confined to a wheelchair.

'I must see you again,' he said entreatingly. 'When *can* I see you?' he repeated with the utmost urgency.

'Can you come back to the ward at dawn?' asked Cynthia in a sublimely encouraging way.

'Indeed I can,' assented Grafton, patting Grandfather Everest on the top of his head and depositing the remainder of the Black Magic on the yellow quilt.

About to walk away, Grafton wheeled around with yet another question:

'Don't some of them die?'

Cynthia smiled. 'All of them do . . . in time.

'Just now I have to look after the others,' she said and disappeared into the atrabilious air.

Grafton entered Gethsemene well before dawn. He was always early for appointments. Grafton knew it was April 10th. He had been so excited he had forgotten it was Mother Everest's birthday. For the first time since he was five he would miss the ritual brushing of hair and bringing Avis morning tea in bed. Poor frail old lady, but the thought of Mother's pained, tight, guilt-inducing face couldn't dampen Grafton's ardour this very special morning.

As he strode the corridors of the old, past rows of drugged and withered inmates, Grafton could hear a strange noise from the private room. He crept up close to the open door. Two robed priests stood in front of an altar saying mass. The altar was draped with the sign of a swastika behind a cross. Incense burned in an open jar. In the middle of the room Tomislav lay naked, imbibing white fluid from a ceremonial chalice. A brilliant crown of gold was on his head; diamonds and amethysts sparkled on his arthritic fingers. Men grouped in threes were holding ancient prayer books and drinking red wine. Two were minus an arm, one a leg, another was totally limbless. In front of the altar was a silver shield and a large black 'U' symbol hung on the wall behind. When the mass had ended, the Gardener, dressed in a uniform embossed with gold braid, went up to the rostrum. He seemed to be presiding. Grafton was transfixed.

The Gardener silenced them with a dramatic sweep of hand. He certainly had style.

'Today is the twenty-eighth anniversary of the establishment of the independent state of Croatia by our beloved Fuhrer, Ante Pavelic.'

The listeners bowed their heads.

'But Pavelic still lives,' intoned the Gardener, pointing to the prostrate Tomislav. 'He lives and reigns over us.' The priests cheered, the others stomped. The old man stirred, limply waved his hand, and collapsed back into unconsciousness.

'He lives in Tomislav our sacred king. Above all he lives in me. I am your ruler and I shall be obeyed,' shrieked the Gardener, his head turned sideways, his jaw thrust out.

Silence fell.

'Today is the beginning of "Operation Punishment".

The glorious Revolutionary Brotherhood will purge our land of all Communists and unbelievers.'

'Death to the dictator Tito.'

'Freedom for our beloved Homeland,' responded the listeners.

The Gardener lifted his hand as if conducting: 'After me brothers.'

'One, two, three . . . Ustasha are we!' chorused the priests. The onlookers joined in and gave the Nazi salute.

Grafton had understood everything that was being said. A specialist in the arcane, he had learnt Serbo-Croat at St Mark's High Anglican Sunday School. He understood everything, and he knew that once more he had stumbled onto something he shouldn't have.

The Gardener silenced the group again, his jewelled hand resting on a Bible embellished in gold and black. As one, those of the men with hands placed them reverently on their books.

'To the Fuhrer, to show him our thanks for all that he has done, for the Croatian people and their liberty, we give this holy oath – the Ustashi oath.'

Grafton listened intently. He had always been a believer. In a high-pitched wail the men repeated:

'I am swearing to Almighty God and all that is holy to me that I will keep to Ustashi principles, and that I will obey all orders and that without question I will keep all my promises and that I will never betray anything.'

Creeping closer to the door, Grafton felt in a fervour.

'I am swearing also that anywhere in the Ustashi ranks, on land or sea, I will fight for Croatian independence and will defend Croatian liberty.

'If I make any mistakes and betray this oath, I am completely aware of my responsibility, and that for every mistake or any misconduct of duty, under the Ustashi law the death penalty is waiting for me.

'So help me God, Amen.'

'Amen,' chorused the group.

'Glory to God and infinite loyalty to the Poglavnik, Dr Ante Pavelic,' incanted the Gardener.

'Sieg Heil!' shouted the listeners and repeated the Nazi salute. Grafton was getting excited.

'For the Homeland. Ready,' responded the circle.

'Za-Dom Spremni,' echoed Grafton from outside the door. His fist was clenched. His arm outraised.

The men were on him. A candle at his eyes, a flick-knife at his testicles.

The Gardener menaced above him. 'Why have you come here? Tell me the truth!' The torturers were closing in.

'To slip it into Cynthia,' Grafton whimpered. The Gardener did not understand. 'To see Dr Old', Grafton stammered piteously. 'I'm in love with Cynthia Old.' At the mention of Cynthia's name, the Gardener removed the knife and flame. 'He is a friend of the good Doctor,' the Gardener explained to the others, who seemed to understand.

The Brotherhood gathered in a huddle, the Gardener again presiding. 'He's so obviously not a Croat . . . yet he speaks the language. He could be of much use,' reasoned the leader. The taller priest nodded sagely.

After the deliberations, the Gardener walked across to Grafton who had not moved a hair.

'I am General Max Lovokovic – Head of the Croatian government in exile. We would like you to join our group.' The Brotherhood expressed its affirmation.

Throughout his life Grafton had felt like the bird on the biscuit tin. Always outside looking in. Now he had a chance to get involved. They seemed sincere enough and they did know Cynthia. 'It might be nice,' Grafton mused, picturing himself standing over Tito's slain form, applauded by the crowds, acclaimed by multitudes.

'I'd be pleased to join,' said Grafton in his best Serbo-Croat. 'It would be an honour.'

'Then meet the Great Brotherhood of Revolutionary Crusaders,' said General Lovokovic, the Gethsemene Gardener.

Grafton was first introduced to Father Janic of the

Church of the Blessed Tavelich and Father Davic, Vicar to the Ustasha Army.

'They have come all the way from Clifton Hill,' said the General as if that explained everything.

'These are my most trusted Ustasha marshals.' As he spoke, Stepan Artukovic of the Black Legion and 'Satnik' Radic, Head of Oceania, stepped forward.

When the General had introduced him to the remaining men, grouped in threes, he put his arm on Grafton's shoulder: 'Ours is an organisation that doesn't exist. Do you understand? This place does not exist. You do not exist. You have seen nothing.' The Revolutionary Crusaders laughed.

'But we musn't keep you from your appointment.' The General winked slyly and held his crotch.

'You will be a great acquisition to the Brotherhood. Rest assured we will be in touch!'

'God and Croatia,' said Grafton and went to stalk bigger game.

As Grafton entered the ward, he felt very powerful. So far it had been an excellent morning.

Cynthia was waiting. She kissed him hungrily on the lips. 'Let's go to my place. It's not really private here.'

Grafton wondered whether Cynthia was making a joke. He glanced at Grandfather's sleeping form and stole two chocolates.

'How are you feeling my darling?' she asked, tenderly taking his arm. As they walked by the drugged old men to Cynthia's third-floor flat at the far end of the hospital grounds, Grafton answered in massive detail. Cynthia's bedroom overlooked the cemetery. 'Some neighbours,' quipped Grafton anxiously looking out the window. 'Doesn't the graveyard make you nervous?'

'I like the dead,' she said. Her eyes glazed.

'Talk to me about death,' pleaded Dr Old, slipping out of her panties. A map of the world and a huge syringe lay by her bed.

Grafton embraced her fearfully, feeling *the place*

moist and dangerous, trying to find *the thing*. He knew where it was from the diagram Avis had drawn him. It's at the top thought Grafton foraging through a forest of wet hair.

'That's nice,' cooed Cynthia: 'O that's very nice. No one's ever done that before.' Grafton's thumb slipped in up to the knuckle. He pulled it out with alarm.

'I'm a virgin,' said Cynthia sadly. 'Thirty-two years old and still a virgin.'

'You don't look your age,' Grafton comforted. That was magic to her ears. Cynthia leant down, removed her teeth, and fished out his cock.

'I'm a virgin too,' confided Grafton earnestly. He didn't tell her about his many forced entrances into the dark back passage. But it was true. He had never entered the place before. He had never touched the thing. It all seemed so very hazardous.

'I can't find it,' said Grafton petulantly, 'I've tried but I just can't. I've felt all up the top and I don't know where it is.'

'That's because it's not there,' said Cynthia, sadder than before.

'Just like the Kikuyu,' said Grafton. 'The elders cut it off so the women can't feel anything and don't go off with other men. Do you know it's a scientific fact that such women gain maximum pleasure from sodomy?'

'I'm hoping for a transplant,' Cynthia continued. She burst into tears.

'Is there anything I can do? ... Anything?' pleaded Grafton in panic. Tears reminded him of Mother. 'Fuck me while I'm asleep,' entreated Cynthia. 'Please.' Cynthia closed her eyes, flicked off the light, injected herself with the syringe and fell into a coma.

Grafton hovered over her, hesitating. The secret odour and darkness excited him beyond belief. His cock however was limp. It will never get hard again thought Grafton. This was a constant fear. Grafton anointed himself with baby oil he had brought for the occasion. Slowly his flaccid member began taking form.

'It'd be like fucking the dead,' mused Grafton, looking out the window and then down at Cynthia again. Inkblot images of talons, thorns and lobster pots surged to mind. Cynthia's cunt became an octopus with tentacles of ice. Grafton trembled. For the first time he entered the place. As he penetrated, deep into forbidden ground, a long low wail came from beneath Cynthia's diaphragm. Her nipples were erect. Still asleep Cynthia rose to meet him. Her body gyrated, her centre slowly circled his staff. With desperate thrusts Grafton kneaded her like clay. His seed was fit for bursting. But could he be carried over? Grafton came like a galaxy. He moaned in glory, and had an asthma attack. Cynthia opened her eyes. They glittered like anthracite.

'I didn't wake you did I?' Grafton wheezed, wiping his cock and adjusting his singlet. His asthma was getting worse.

'Oh, my darling,' said Cynthia, 'you did it while I slept.' Grafton bowed his head.

'I have to go now,' whimpered Grafton, thinking of Mother and regretting what he had done.

'You're clean, aren't you?' he asked in a hushed voice.

'Of course I am,' said Dr Old.

'Don't worry, you're in good hands,' reassured Cynthia, buttoning his fly. 'The Brotherhood will be in touch.'

Grafton could hardly believe his eyes. A Centurion tank with its nozzle raised was circling the hospital grounds. An Australian Army sergeant was at the wheel. Men dressed like stormtroopers were firing blanks from bazookas and throwing hand grenades at a mock-up of President Tito from behind barbed-wire barricades. Grafton had seen them all in Tomislav's room – save one. In the middle of the grounds, supervising the proceedings from an elaborate wheel-chair, was a limbless Croat with medals all over his torso. He seemed to swagger sitting down. As Grafton approached to get a closer look he realized that all was hidden from public gaze by the rows of poplar trees around the Old Men's Home. Gethsemene mood music turned up to eighty decibels blotted out the sound.

'We've been waiting for you to begin,' said limbless Dr Makic, the former concentration camp commandant now President of the Croatian Soccer Club. In response to an imperious gesture of his chin, the men lined up on parade. They listened intently as he spoke.

'Our other missions to liberate the Homeland failed because we were unmanly and unprepared.' Grafton dimly recalled the abortive invasions of '72 and '75.

'But this time Tito will die. The Croatian Army of our Revolutionary Brotherhood will be victorious. Zagreb will be free.'

As one, the men threw their bayonets into the air and cheered. Dr Makic silenced them.

'Drinking, taking drugs, playing games with your co-fighters is out of the question and will be severely punished. We Croats do not drink wine; we drink the blood of the Serb, the Jew, the Orthodox and the Communist traitors.

'Trust no-one,' Dr Makic screamed. 'Beware of co-conspirators . . . The Secret Police are everywhere,' he announced meaningfully. 'Let us repeat our oath and go.'

Sombrely the men recited the Holy Kletva and left in threes.

After the men dispersed, Dr Makic, summoning Grafton, self-propelled himself to the Gethsemene operating theatre. Grafton followed as bidden. Cynthia and the Gardener were waiting.

Inside the Theatre was a cache – gelignite, fuses, detonators, time-bombs, explosives, walkie-talkies, booby-traps and bazookas. Grafton was amazed. 'You see we are well-prepared,' said Dr Makic. 'Your role is of the utmost importance,' counselled the Gardener. Cynthia nodded and took Grafton off to bed.

*   *   *

In the weeks that followed there was much to be done. Instructed by Sergeant Wodonga of the Australian Tank Corps and Dr Makic, Grafton received extensive para-military training. Individual terror, sabotage, subversion and acts of violence were the order of the day. His obesity and essential sloth rendered things difficult at first. But Grafton was an excellent student. He followed every instruction to the letter. Soon he began to excel. With the aid of Dr Makic's diagram, Grafton made his first incendiary bomb. Every night Cynthia brought him into line, coercing him to explore each orifice of her tall and supple form.

Grafton was the chief of his troika; Father Janic, an ingenious man, was the intelligence officer; a third member was the mine layer and explosives expert. They lost a number of number threes. An enthusiastic young Croat blew his legs off trying to bomb the Yugoslav Consulate, while Stepan Artukovic of the Black Legion detonated himself at the Soccer finals. Eventually it was decided that the Gardener himself would be the mine layer. He made no mistakes. Grafton, the priest and the Gardener-General forged themselves into an excellent team. On a last-night excursion they terrorized Tito supporters at the Serbia Club and, using Grafton's incendiary bomb, set fire to the Yugoslav People's Palace. While they were practising, Father Davic was saying a requiem mass for a member of another team.

At the final briefing it was explained that seventeen of the loyal Australian Brotherhood would invade the Homeland from Austria. Crossing the western mountains of Croatia they would rendezvous with other invading forces and representatives of the Government-in-Exile from Argentina and Spain. The place chosen was Varazdin on the River Drava. The surrounding hills are perfect for protracted guerilla warfare. The Australian wing of the Croatian Revolutionary Brotherhood under the Gardener-General's direct command was to be disguised as a male choir on a cultural exchange. From Sydney International Airport until they reached

Zagreb, Grafton was to be their official leader and choirmaster. He was tone deaf.

The brotherhood, who had left Gethsemene by ambulance, gathered at the terminal. Among the crowd of crippled, maimed and limbless, Grafton stood erect in the Thai Air departure lounge, clutching a fake passport, a songbook and his koala bear. Snugly fitted inside the toy animal were a detonator, a silencer and a stick of dynamite. Similarly stood the other choristers. Some held wombats, others kangaroos. Cynthia, the group physician and chaperone, carried a platypus. All the animals were filled with explosives, ammunition, fuses and small arms. The rifles and larger weaponry were packed in cello and violin cases that stood by the excess luggage counter. Grafton conducting, the group sang 'Jesu Joy of Man's Desiring' in slow and stilted English. Head bowed, hands trembling at the occasion, Grafton announced in his best Serbo-Croat: 'Our Mission will succeed. With the guidance of God victory is ours.' The other passengers looked bemused.

Seated next to Cynthia in the 747, Grafton felt amazingly powerful. At his beloved's request, the frail Thai hostess brought him a bowl of mushroom soup. 'That's just what you need,' said Cynthia. Looking around him, head erect, Grafton knew he was going to be famous. Everything was fitting into place. He decided that after this adventure he would marry Cynthia and settle down. As the aircraft taxied down the runway everything became a chaos of light.

'Do you think Avis will mind?' Grafton said out loud. 'I should have let her know.'

'I'm sure she'll be very proud of you. Have some more soup,' Cynthia coaxed. 'It'll do you the world of good.'

'At least I'm *participating*,' proclaimed Grafton from the window seat. 'At least. I'm ...' Grafton lifted his weary head which nodded back again. His fat hand reached out very slowly for the plastic spoon. 'Those clouds are so ... beautiful,' he yawned at the swirling white nimbus outside. 'I've never felt at home in the world.' Grafton's voice seemed far away. 'At best I seem like a visitor.' He felt sleepier and sleepier.

Having begun, the flight did not seem to end. Grafton was on the banks of the River Drava. A thin member of the Yugoslav Secret Police was beating him with a pistol. 'Why did you come here? Why?' Grafton saw all the dead Brotherhood scattered around him. He was totally naked, tethered to a stake. Cynthia and the Gardener were smiling, holding hands, looking on. What had gone wrong? In a flash it dawned: Cynthia was an agent. It had all been planned. He had been fooled again. But what had he done? Grafton shook his sweating head. He'd just wanted to get involved. Snow was falling on the bare Croatian hills. A pack of wolves approached from the river bank. There was a whirlpool of vomit and blood.

'The Lord is my shepherd,' cried Grafton. 'He maketh me lie down in green pastures. He leadeth me beside still waters.'

'Welcome to Gethsemene,' sang the Gardener and smiled.

The wolves closed in, ripping and tearing in a baptism of blood. Grafton was being eaten from the feet up.

'Trust no-one,' said Cynthia.

The lead wolf licked his chops and gobbled Grafton's mutilated head.

'Trust no-one,' repeated Cynthia, looking deep into the Gardener's clear and twinkling eyes. 'Not anybody.'

The Knight

It was the day before the Queen's Birthday. Wearing the
frog-green bathers Mother had bought him for his birthday, Grafton was sitting by the pool cleaning his shoes.
He did them once a year. No prisoner of the hours, Che
Guevara, the Burmese, was in the garden chasing liz-
ards. A smart cat, Che knew when to keep her distance.
Nursing a nipped ankle, Grafton was ruminating about
the perils of wealth and fame. The automatic apple
picker hadn't quite worked. It had grappled Enrico
Mattea's trees with such force that it almost ripped
them out of the ground. When the catching device collapsed, instead of cushioning and sorting the fruit softly
as they fell, the machine went wild, pulverizing the
apples into a purée. The last thing the inventor could
remember was the Italian orchardist's black-and-white
kelpie bitch setting after him . . . and Mr Mattea, white
with rage.

In theory the machine ran on fuel made from the
apples it discarded – the rest it picked and packed without bruising. A self-perpetuating apple picker! That
would get his name in the papers. Converting the sugar
in the apples to fuel, in a fermentation machine smaller
than a tank, was Grafton's big problem. So far the
machine just gobbled up all the apples Grafton fed it. If
the truth be known the self-perpetuating machine was
beginning to bore him. His white arms covered in Nugget,
Grafton reached for the weekend *Australian*. He felt it
kept him in touch.

The Honours List headed the news. Emblazoned on

the top right quarter of the front page, above the usual assortment of bishops and politicians, was a blurred photograph of Henry Müller, the industrial entrepreneur. Henry had been awarded a KCMG. Sir Henry must really be creaming himself this morning Grafton ruminated, rubbing Che behind the ears. 'It can't be that hard to get a knighthood,' he announced to the Burmese who sulkily shook her head and ran away. 'I'd settle for a KBE or even a plain Knights Bachelor. I just want to be a Sir.' Grafton had so far browned one shoe.

The Nobel Prize was tarnished these days, even with the money. And Grafton hadn't really wanted to write, he just wanted to be a writer. Yes, a knighthood was much more his cup of tea. Sir Grafton and Lady Everest. First things first. He'd find himself a bride after the ordination. Grafton left the remaining shoes, had a glass of flavoured milk and took Che off for their morning nap. 'Musn't get overhungry, overtired or overthirsty,' he repeated to himself. 'Grafton Everest, KBE, for distinguished services to national security, and the Commonwealth.' That sounded sufficiently mysterious, yet at the same time clear. 'No comment' he mumbled in his sleep and smiled.

He woke with a start. There must be someone who types the final list. A secretary. The secretary to the Private Secretary to the PM. I could find out who she is, win her heart and she'd put me on. 'That wouldn't work,' he grumbled, reaching for the Multivite. 'With my luck she'd be too old or a dyke. Anyway someone higher up would always check and they'd find me out.

'It'd have to be more direct,' he continued, out loud, mixing a glass of Sustagen and cutting raw liver for the cat. Like a call to the P.M. from the Queen. 'This is Buckingham Palace. Hello Prime Minister. It was absolutely *wonderful* to see you last year. I'm just phoning to say congratulations. A little late I know . . . O you are too kind. And to ask a very small favour. You know what trouble I've been having with Andrew don't you? He gets into all sorts of *terribly* embarrassing scraps . . . One of your Australian chaps has just been absolutely *wonderful* to Andy – and I just want to reward him in some small and trivial way. Indirectly, of course . . . That was *exactly* what I had in mind. No, not the highest. That would stand out like . . . (Yes, I am rather coy.) The ermine robe won't be necessary. The name is Everest, Grafton Everest . . . Somewhere in Brisbane, actually. The occupation *is* a little embarrassing. So let's put "Retired". He's thirty-three and single. Please make sure that my name is kept out of it. Make absolutely certain it seems to come from you. No, no correspondence at all . . . You are a dear. And if I can help *you* in any way, please don't hesitate to ring.'

Grafton, who had just read about the young Lionel Barrymore reciting Hamlet's 'drown the stages with tears' speech over and over again in front of a mirror, acted out the Royal part with great enthusiasm. He looked at his naked and very white self in the mirror, swallowed the rest of his Sustagen and frowned. But he'd know the voice. He's eaten with her . . . Grafton went to his desk and thought. There must be *someone* in Australia who can imitate the Queen. There is in England. It's only the voice that's needed. There's probably some old sheila doing the clubs right now. She can't be too hard to track down. All this thought exhausted him. Time to start to look after the body. Switching the phone to 'Record' and leaving the pussy door open, Grafton put on his new running shoes and struggled into the midday air. Perhaps exercise might help?

The black man on the bicycle followed Grafton as he laboriously navigated the park. He plodded on the tan reserved for horses while the man traversed the bitumen path outside. Running was good for the mind. Mother had told him so. Yet why was he so *tired*? And why was Prester John following, at lunchbreak? Round and round the park, smiling, stroking with his eyes. A prim, fastidious figure, Grafton had seen him at the Club talking with Feydor Shelyapin, Grafton's supervisor.

They spoke in fluent Russian. The Corporation had brought Prester all the way from Botswana to bring the boys into line. Grafton had warned them on the first day. Someone who touches is not to be trusted. He had told them so.

Sweat streaming from his eyes, Grafton could stand it no longer. He stopped in his tracks, waddled up demanding an explanation: 'Why are you following me? I'm on R-and-R.' Prester John lifted his lithe black body off the bicycle and took Grafton by the arm, gently at first, but firmly, pulling, looking Grafton straight in the eyes. 'Tell me the truth,' Grafton pleaded. Still holding him, now stroking, Prester laughed. 'Honestly man, only the really paranoid want to know the truth.'

Prester got back on his bike. 'Friend, you and I are going places. Be packed and ready at noon tomorrow.' Breathless on the tan, Grafton was very much the worse for wear. 'Why did I get into this business in the first place?' he lamented on the phone to Avis, who knew.

They flew to M'bwane, capital of Swaziland, then drove the car, a clapped-out Volvo with Durban plates, carefully towards the border, avoiding springboks and impalas which occasionally ran beside. Grafton was amazed by the signs: 'Danger, Elephants Crossing' . . . 'Drive carefully, 200 people have been killed on this road in the last four years'. At the Goba border-post Prester eased him through customs. 'How are things, camarada, now that the Portuguese are gone?' The official shrugged his shoulders. 'It's the same pile of manure,' he smiled wearily, 'only the flies are different.' Although stopped seven times in seventy kilometres by eager young Frelimo militiamen, all armed with machine guns, they had a pleasant drive into Maputo. The outlying houses were still in Portuguese pastels, lush tropical trees arched over wide avenues. The early evening air was sultry and very still. Beside the road, billboards featuring garish pictures of black workers brandishing hoes, fists and rifles were stickered with slogans in red, green and yellow: 'Long live our great

71

friend Samora Machel,' 'The war continues,' 'We will not rest until all Africa is free'. As they approached the capital, Grafton noticed that there were no people in the streets, only abandoned cars and garbage. Half finished buildings were everywhere, some with their cranes still standing. The streets were full of potholes; once flowering parks were brown.

They drove to the Hotel Turisimo, an opulent white and lavender palace constructed at the height of the Lourenco Marques tourist trade. Overlooking the Indian Ocean, it was built for the very rich. Before '74 the building industry had been booming and Maputo becoming one of the world's great resorts. Now the hotel was almost empty. Although the occasional Russian and Bulgarian technician ambled through the corridors, there was not one Western European to be seen. The ornate baroque building was falling into ruins. There was no painting on the walls, except slogans. No maintenance work was being done at all; maize grew on the terraces. The porter, a black boy from Pembo, met them at the lobby and carried Prester's suitcase up five flights of stairs. The lifts weren't working. As a gesture of solidarity, Grafton carried his own. 'How are things here?' he asked. 'The lifts don't work,' replied the porter, making sure no one else heard. 'There's no running water anywhere in town. But the roads to Zimbabwe are good,' he said with a smile.

Suares Machava, the Frelimo official, a small bearded man sporting a monocle, met them at the hotel's croquet lawn. With him was an exquisitely pretty white youth wearing a Panama hat and Bermuda shorts. In his right hand he held a mallet. The boy's face was androgynous, his eyes misty royal blue. They walked to the beach, the official shaking his tiny fist and shouting vengeance against Ian Smith and all enemies of Scientific Socialism in passable French. Prester nodded. The youth, who said nothing, was introduced as Burgess Maclean. It seemed an unlikely name. Grafton could scarcely keep his eyes off him. 'Camarada, tomorrow is

25 June, Independence Day,' explained Machava.
'Tomorrow we invade.' They walked back to the
Turisimo and with a tired sigh Prester ordered dry mar-
tinis, and a tomato juice for Grafton. Grafton's face
turned white and ill. 'Molto grazie,' he said in desperation as Prester proposed a toast. 'To the invasion.'
Grafton raised his glass unsteadily, as if in shock. 'Don't
worry,' said Burgess, reaching out and gently touching
his plump arm. He let it rest there. 'You're with me.'
They were the first words Grafton had heard him say.
The accent was clearly English upper class – probably
schooled at Gordonstun or Eton. A smiling portrait of
Samora Machel looked down upon them. 'It can't be all
that bad,' thought Grafton, concentrating on the youth.
'I wonder who he really is.'

After a late breakfast of prawns, milk and malaria
pills served on an off-white tablecloth with real silver
and chipped crystal, Grafton announced his intentions
to Burgess. 'Before we go, let's sample some local hard-
ware.' Not quite understanding, the youth agreed.
When they left the hotel it was high noon. They caught
one of the five taxis still operating in Maputo and drove
to the oldest part of town. Although it was siesta, queues
of people, clutching ration cards, waited outside the
shops. The last time soap had been available was in
November. Maputo hadn't seen a tomato in months. The
whore house was eleven stories high, and they walked
up, one by one. Men bleeding from the nostrils drank
booze that smelt like arak. Vacant-eyed young girls
covered in mosquitoes stood half-naked at each opening,
waiting. Grafton selected his prey, a middle-aged
mulatto, and fucked her face to face, rocking chair fash-
ion, while the boy looked on. 'I'm thirty-three years old
and there's no one in the world I love,' she cried in
Portuguese. 'If it's any consolation I'm in exactly the
same boat. We all are aren't we?' Grafton said, coming
weakly and turning to the boy. The woman had disappointed him. They were always less in the flesh. Burgess
behind her, the mulatto looked up in alarm. Turning

round Grafton saw Prester with a raised machete in his hand. I must get up to save the boy. As he ran, Burgess disappeared into a milky haze. Grafton fell dazed down the stairs. The eleven storeys kaleidoscoped into the street. Prester bent over, picked him up and carried him like a child. They were driven direct to the docks in a white car marked 'Estado'. Prester didn't say a word.

The SS *Beira*, supposedly carrying cashew nuts, was manned by a most unlikely crew. The captain was a Jewish bookmaker who looked much like Feydor Shelyapin. Dressed in identical ill-fitting uniforms and wearing Castro berets, Prester, Grafton and silent Burgess, now carrying a thermos flask and picnic lunch in a Japanese basket, sailed up the Limpopo, destination West Nicholson and from there through Gwelo to Salisbury. The others, some 640 kilometres up the coast, would take the Zambezi and go down on Salisbury from Lusaka. So this is where the elephant got its trunk, Grafton thought as they sailed the murky waters. The invasion didn't seem to be dangerous at all. Looking overboard he saw royal blue peacocks floating by. The sky above was crimson.

As they steamed towards Botswana, a swarm of golden butterflies engulfed the ship. 'They're suicidal,' announced Grafton. 'Suicidal butterflies. Swarms more will come.' The sky was a descending carpet of petals. 'Jump overboard,' he screamed at Burgess who obeyed. 'Swim with the current.' Looking back he saw the ship surrounded in gold. The rest of the crew would suffocate, but they were safe. Grafton lifted the youth out of reach of a hungry crocodile. To render it harmless he prized its mouth apart with a stick. 'That was the kindest thing anyone has ever done for me,' said Burgess, wading out of the river and shaking Grafton warmly by the hand. 'You're a prince,' he said and laughed.'You saved my life.'

Two smiling plainclothes men flashed Frelimo badges and entered the room. Both asked questions in rapid English. Why were they here? What was Grafton's occupation? Who was the boy? Whose side was he on? They tasted the Bonox heating on a primus, examined every scrap of paper in the room. The small man who looked like Suares Machava hit Grafton over and over again on the head with a blunt instrument. He asked the same question: Who was the boy? A knife was inserted between Grafton's tied fingers and twisted, his knuckles cut and pried apart. Still he did not speak. A guard held his face over a spike while the smiling men danced on his shoulders. 'I am thirty-three years old and there's no one in the world I love,' he sobbed. 'Above all be truthful,' said the nurse injecting a syringe in his temple. 'Who is the boy?'

'He is a prince,' Grafton screamed, 'a prince. Let him go,'

'You've saved his life,' said Machava, and left.

Grafton lay dazed on the tan. Blood ran down his nostrils. Mother Everest had Che on a leash. At last Grafton comprehended. It was she who did the clubs. It was Mother who impersonated the Queen. Her fingers moist, Avis hovered over him, wiping his face, bandaging his scarred and swollen hands. What else didn't he know about her? 'It won't be long my son,' she said without a single tear in her eye.

'When will the knighthood come?' Grafton moaned, clutching at the boy. Jacarandas, with their scented wood and mauve flowers, swayed in the breeze. Feydor and Burgess from the factory had come to pay a visit. It was too late. Vacant-eyed like the girls, Grafton was waiting on the Lord. 'He's dead. He's really dead,' the doctor said. The orderly wheeled him quietly away.

Che the cat rolled on her back, pretty paws in the air. Mother Everest stroked its chinny-chin-chin and smiled. She knew. Real people always interfere with our image of them. Always.

III

Good luck, old son.
Anthony Aloysius St John Hancock

The Introduction

Richard's grandfather was Sir Clarence Cropps – a benevolent socialist and member of the Wartime Labour Cabinet. The Indian radio announcer had called him Sir Clorence Crapps and lost his job. His father, a Queen's Counsellor and Peer of the Realm, was an unbending, unbenevolent Tory. His three elder brothers had gone from Eton to Oxford to the bar. Richard was the only dunce.

Having glandular trouble, Richard had been enormously fat since he was very young. From as far back as he could remember he was thought to be stupid.

'Stupid. Cropps, you're stupid.'

'S.T.U.P.I.D,' incanted the Classics Master.

'Can you spell that backwards?'

'No sir,' whimpered Dicky. The small rich boys, aristocrats all, laughed and jeered.

'That's because you're stupid,' the master thundered, throwing young Richard a butterfly net.

'Catch me a butterfly, you wretched boy.' It was the middle of winter. While the others decoded 'The Rape of the Sabine Women' or waded through Petrarchan odes, Richard ran in tears, net in hand, round and round the playing fields of Eton. Or traversed the lower oval three times backwards for not doing his sums. Or jerked off, alone and dreamlessly, in the upper dormitories at night.

With Herculean determination and almost blinded by late-night swatting, Richard never quite failed at school. Friendlessly he scraped through his finals but – and this hung very heavily on him – he did not make the Varsity. He had to go to the City instead.

Richard became an accountant and, with the aid of his father's friends, a very rich one. As his middle twenties limped by, RC was still fat (though through the aid of rigorous diet no longer obese), still regarded by his family (but not his clientele) as stupid, and decidedly devoid of female company. After the latter there was no parenthesis.

In an outward sense he was comfortable. Dressed in a pin-striped suit he could be seen situated every luncheon and early afternoon, in White's Club, a gin and tonic in his right hand, an Havana cigar in the left, talking about grouse and the hounds with Lord Curzon and the lesser lights, and the iniquities of the Welfare State with anyone who'd care to listen. In the evening he went home to Mummy and Daddy out of town, played dominoes and cribbage, and slowly ate his only substantial meal. Having been brought up mainly by a nanny, Richard was very much in awe of his parents.

A very respectable young man was Cropps. He voiced all the proper opinions in a sufficiently monosyllabic way never to seem a threat. He was, in other words, perfectly acceptable.

His only known abnormality was that he believed in astrology. (Privately he wrote romantic sonnets in Latin.) Every week he went to see his fortune teller – a thin, domineering woman with eyes like tea leaves – and followed her instructions (she called them prophecies) to the letter. 'Never associate with gypsies.' 'Stay with Standard Oil.' 'Avoid women until you're thirty.' Richard followed *that* piece of exacting advice with such an obsessional enthusiasm that he not only remained womanless but was rendered entirely without sexual desire of any kind. Up to now the teller's instructions had all proved profitable. To Richard, the only thing extraordinary about her utterances was the prediction of his coming fame. This she repeated at every session and Richard listened with interest and respect.

Out of the blue, and without pausing after her stock exchange analysis, the teller announced 'You are to study political science at Case Western Reserve University.' A half-opened copy of the *New Statesman* lay on her desk.

'Where is that?' asked Dicky in a quite matter-of-fact old-Etonian tone.

'In Cleveland, Ohio,' the thin woman answered. 'It's a wealthy, private establishment.' As it happened, Dr Spock and Erich Fromm taught there.

The next day Richard closed his office and flew to Cleveland. He took a taxi straight to the campus, ignoring the encroaching ghettos as he went.

The Chairman of the school was Reynard de Quincy, another Englishman of baronial descent – albeit Norman – and very eccentric habits. He had married three times in the last two years. The third marriage lasted five days.

'What brings you here?' asked Professor de Quincy as Richard's seventeen stone of aristocratic manhood ambled in.

'Why, my astrologer,' replied Cropps without batting an eye.

'How grand,' pronounced Reynard, thumbing through Richard's curriculum vitae. What a bizarre sense of humour this chap has . . . and plenty of money too. 'Welcome to Case Western,' smiled Reynard with a lordly wave of hand. Richard was *in*. He was given five units of credit for his accountancy courses and immediate enrolment. 'Do come and have a drink.'

They walked to Jimmy's private bar in the Commodore Hotel. It was here Richard met Grafton, an ex-student of Reynard's who had inveigled his way into a number of rich and prestigious postgraduate awards. Wild-eyed and sucking on a double dacquiri, Reynard's only prodigy perched unsteadily on a barstool as Richard was introduced.

'What do you do, old chap?' RC asked.

'I write poems and try to fuck sheilas,' said Grafton,

81

playing The Australian to the hilt. 'And the odd bloke too, if the truth be known,' he roared, patting Dicky's ample behind. He drinks too much and far too quickly, Richard thought. An interesting fellow but very much beneath my station. He was obviously poor.

The professor of anthropology, a Tamil from Madras, entered the bar, ordered a small tonic and lemon and made a beeline for Reynard. He started explaining the ills of the world, entirely oblivious of the other patrons. Richard listened intently as he expounded his theory of cosmic payback with a furrowed brow.

'You get nothing for nothing,' announced the anthropologist. 'Take what you want from the universe, but pay.' The notion of cosmic payback made enormous sense to Richard. He thought of his brothers and the boys at school. The rest didn't seem impressed. During a lull in the monologue Cropps felt he had to add encouragement.

'You know, you're a remarkably intelligent chap for an Indian,' Richard beamed. Silence struck the group. Dicky had made his mark.

Although regarded by the faculty as somewhat strange, Richard proceeded unimpeded through his degree. Case Western had a system of self-grading until graduate school. Richard always graded himself B. As a result his work went entirely unnoticed until he had to submit his first written exercise. Cropp's Foreign Policy piece was entitled 'The Influence of Asteroid Orbits on the Korean War' – replete with page after page of charts and diagrams.

'He really believes this crap,' lamented Marty Bowen, his MA instructor, to the chairman of the school. 'What the fuck are we going to do with him?' Reynard de Quincy shrugged his shoulders and went off to join Grafton for a morning drink. No one had failed at Case since he'd taken command. No one ever would.

America brought out the best in Dicky. He opened up. While somewhat of an embarrassment inside the school, he soon became the leader of the Radical Right outside. He started making speeches, a peculiar amalgam of Burke, Cicero and Mr Enoch Powell, in his stout lordly way, manifesting a paternal concern for those less fortunate than himself. This and his entirely unselfconscious racism were a quickfire guarantee of success. When the blacks burnt down half of Euclid Avenue and most of the campus, Richard appeared on NBC TV with Mayor Carl Stokes. Asked to explain the riots, Richard blinked in puzzlement, looked straight into the camera and said, 'Funny, they're usually such happy folk.'

In a fit of flamboyancy Reynard made Grafton and Richard graduate assistants. They were to teach separate, but interlocking, strands in Introductory American Government. Instead of the Supreme Court and Congress, Richard bombarded his group with Virgil, Homer and Wordsworth, while Grafton, always three quarters drunk, preached a subversive brand of anarchic individualism to his. They met twice a week to compare notes. Proximity, and pooling their ignorance, brought them very close. The two assistants could often be seen parading around the campus, arm in arm – Richard straight and regal, Grafton slouched – reciting poems in tandem to anyone who'd care to listen. One night at a particularly lyrical moment, Richard brought his portly arm around the Australian, looked at him earnestly and said, 'I can't understand why we're such good friends, Everest. After all, you're working class.'

One of Grafton's students was Mary Jane – a small-breasted, six-foot Fundamentalist Southern Baptist. She too was of the lower orders. Mary Jane was extremely virginal and very straight. During class she seldom said a word. Not surprisingly, Grafton took a perverse interest in her. He fantasized many a night away thinking of what he'd do to her, and how, and where. One afternoon, as she walked past the Commodore, Grafton lurched out and summoned her to the pictures that night. Too thunderstruck to say no, Mary Jane acquiesced.

Grafton plied her with booze, but finished up drinking it

all himself. Instead of the movies he took her straight to the flat in Little Italy – a most unsalubrious whites-only area – which he shared with Bill, an old railroad worker who was away on yet another jag. Dirty underwear and half-empty flagons of claret littered the floor. The only food visible was a tiny jar of Vegemite which he'd purchased out of loyalty and at great expense from the international delicatessen. Neglecting the preliminaries, Grafton rushed at the mystified Mary and tried to tear off her panties. The student was even stronger than she looked. Approaching him front on she bearhugged Grafton and almost squeezed him lifeless. Then she kicked him under the crutch, just missing the vitals. This treatment galvanized Everest. Winded, but excited beyond belief, the Australian exposed himself, pointing at his half-erect member in a deaf-mute way. Mary saw the swelling thing and ran wild-eyed and screaming through the door ... right into the aristocratic open arms of Richard Windsor Cropps, who was making his first social call since Grafton had shifted from the ghetto. Richard held her tight. Mary Jane pressed, sobbing, against his ample breast as Grafton appeared, bloodied and smiling, buttoning up his pants.

'This is disgusting, Grafton,' said Dicky, surveying the squalor and using his Richard voice. He left taking Mary by the hand. Two weeks before Richard had turned thirty and took this to be a sign.

Something deep had been awoken in his lordly heart. Richard's ardour had been stirred. In earnest he began his courtship of Mary Jane. Sitting alone on her bed in the once-sterile dormitory, Mary was amazed – her room was full of flowers. In her hands was a bunch of telegrams. All said the same thing: 'MARRY ME STOP I ADORE YOU STOP RICHARD'. Red roses and forget-me-nots flowed into the hall. Was last night a dream? she asked herself as she went to answer a knock at the door. A sophomore stood open-mouthed at the top of the stairs. 'He's on the phone again.'

. 'Marry me,' Richard implored, 'I adore you.' 'Marry me,' he repeated in a manic tone.

Richard was single-minded in his pursuit. A week ensued and he telephoned every day. Richard never asked her out but twice daily he sent around flowers by courier and a proposal on a printed card. 'Marry me' was begining to sound like an order. Having always done as she was told, Mary Jane was finding it hard to refuse. With every proposal he attached a poem – always a sonnet in Latin, which she couldn't read. What mysterious messages did they contain? Mary Jane was nonplussed as she tried to decipher the words. All that she could understand was Richard's name at the bottom of each page.

In desperation (and having a forgiving nature) she rang Grafton. In the circumstances he was the only one she could turn to. 'Is this guy for real?' she cried into the telephone. 'I'm afraid so,' answered the Australian. 'He's flipped his load for you.' Grafton was mixing metaphors but the meaning was plain enough. 'I can't hack this pressure,' pined Mary Jane, '. . . and those poems.' Then she paused, 'He'll tire of me soon, I hope.' Her voice turned warm and quiet.

Every day flowers and cables came, the telephone rang, his proposal was repeated. Above all there were poems. Within two months Richard had vanity-pressed a book of verse. *The Love Poems of Virgil Scott* he called them, edited, translated and with an introduction by himself. Every poem was entitled 'To Mary'. Fifty copies arrived at the door, accompanied by a bouquet of orchids. Mary Jane was overwhelmed. 'No one wrote me poems before,' she said shyly viewing the fat Englishman's photograph which filled the entire back cover. 'And, after all, he is a handsome man.' Richard had worn her down.

With trembling hands she reached for the telephone. Richard's recorded voice answered, 'If you wish to leave a message wait until three pips sound, and then proceed.' Mary put the receiver to her lips. 'Yes', she whispered without restraint. There were tears in her eyes. 'Yes. Yes. Yes.'

Having won his prize, Richard faced only one big problem. His MA was drawing to a close. Soon he would return to England. A week after their engagement the awful reality seeped in. Mary Jane would have to meet Mummy and Daddy. Worse, they would have to meet his bride to be. Richard realized he hadn't mentioned a word of her. Although *he* didn't feel it, to the unseeing eye Mary Jane didn't seem to be his class. What would Mummy and Daddy say? Would they let him marry?

Mary had to be prepared. Richard gave her an embossed copy of *Lady Troubridge's Book of Etiquette* and told her to learn it off by heart. There was only a month until they had to leave Case Western. Mary abandoned her course and began a whirlwind of elocution and bridge lessons, dressing, dance and table instruction. Mary Jane tried very hard to please her man. Every night she and Richard practised in the dormitory for the big event – Richard playing the part of Mummy, Daddy and the head servant as well. There was nowhere else in Cleveland they could try a test run. As Richard was at pains to explain, there was nothing in America quite like a dinner party at Mummy and Daddy's house.

'Welcome home, Mr Richard,' mumbled the head servant opening the drawing-room door and bowing low. The best of the family were inside. Under the chandelier Richard's eldest brother Tyrell and his wife were sipping sherry with Sir John and Lady Tredear. The Marquis and Marchioness of Coke huddled in the corner with Lord and Lady Lamington. By the gold grandfather clock Great Aunt Laura and Vera de Vere were discussing quail. The room seemed full of mirrors. Mary Jane was petrified.

A tall, straight woman with ample bosom moved forward to greet them. She wore a long royal-blue lace evening gown and a rope of very large baroque pearls.

Her grey hair, swept up high, was clasped in jade; two huge diamonds embellished her fingers. Timidly taking Mary's hand Richard stammered, 'Mamma, this is my special friend.' Lady Cropps fixed directly on Mary Jane's engagement ring and said slowly, 'Hmmm.' Richard's father, a small man, wore a monocle and black tie. He smiled benignly and took Mary in to dinner.

The long table was set for fourteen. Mary was placed between Richard's father and Lord Lamington. Sitting opposite, beside his mother, Richard seemed far away. Four underservants, white napkins above their arms, brought more sherry and Portuguese soup. Exquisite crystal was on display. The family silver, adorned with the Cropps' crest, was clearly to be used. There would be at least five courses. Seeing the confusion of cutlery beneath her, Mary's mind went white. What did Lady Troubridge say? 'Go from the outside in,' she repeated and gripped the spoon.

Lord Lamington was charming in an unobtrusive way. By the time the filets de sole and white burgundy came, Mary started warming up. Soon Richard was signalling his betrothed to be silent. He was in a particularly black humour having been given a dietary serving specially prepared by his mother. It reminded him of infancy.

Beginning to relax, Mary relapsed into holding her knife and fork in an ungenteel Fundamental way. Richard winced visibly. He knew Mamma was watching.

'Tell me about your family, my dear,' prompted Lord Lamington.

'We're Baptists,' Mary Jane said sweetly. 'Mother stays at home and my father's a butcher.'

'He's not *really* a butcher, Mamma,' interrupted Richard. 'More of an entrepreneur actually . . . And her uncle's an Anglican,' he added as an after-thought. Mary Jane glanced down at the plush carpet and bit her tongue.

Avoiding her fiancé's frown, Mary tucked gustily into the quail. 'Wow, this quail pudding is superb,' Mary Jane enthused, 'I'd love a second helping.'

Richard raised a fat hand and mouthed across the table, 'One never asks for more.' All the family could see what he was doing. They turned to witness her reply.

Something seemed to snap. Mary Jane screamed, 'I want some more ... M.O.R.E,' she shouted at eighty decibels, pounding each letter on the mahogany table with the back of her antique fork. 'Get me more,' she cried and burst into a torrent of tears.

Richard scurried away from the table and brought her a monstrous helping. 'Here you are, my darling precious,' he whimpered and kissed her on the cheek.

'Thank you,' replied Mary. She seemed remarkably composed.

'That's the way to deal with our Dicky,' said the great lady with a twinkle in her eyes. 'My dear, you're very welcome in our home.'

'Indeed you are,' assented Great Aunt Laura.

'We must discuss the wedding,' said Lady Cropps, taking her future daughter-in-law warmly by the arm.

The rest of the family departed without dessert.

Dicky would be thirty-one in two months time. The future didn't look auspicious.

Otters

'Ever had a job?'

'Only once,' drawled Ken, sucking deeply on a Dunhill. 'I went down to Sydney for the Cup. Won a packet.' He exhaled a haze of smoke. 'But I got *pissed* and lost my money in the surf. Tried to pawn my towel at the Cross. They wouldn't be in it. So I bludged the night with some sheila and jumped the ferry to Taronga Park Zoo; landed a job feeding the otters.

'They're lovely little animals, otters.' Ken spoke with a gentleness Grafton hadn't heard before. He lit another Dunhill.

'After I'd fed them, there I was shovelling up the otter shit, when a bloke called out, "Hey you, you can take your time".'

'I *am* taking me time,' Ken replied, resting hugely on the shovel.

' "No. Take your fucking time!" said the voice. "Piss off. You're fired." I got sacked before lunchtime.'

Ken wheezed and looked thoughtful. 'If I get sober,' he said deliberately, 'I think I'd like to work with animals.'

'Otter feeders aren't exactly in demand in Brisbane!', Grafton responded, serving dinner. Ken's lacklustre eyes shimmered a little.

'But who knows what might happen if you stay sober.'

Before eating, Ken produced a bottle of pancreatitis pills and swallowed ten gigantic white tablets. 'If I don't do that,' he explained, 'I can't digest a fucking thing.'

'If *I* had pancreatitis,' said Dr Lewisham when Grafton told him of Ken's death, 'I'd neck myself. I really would. The pain is appalling. There's nothing one can do.'

'What are you doing tonight?' Grafton asked three weeks before Ken died.

'I've got to take some dog out. So I can't go to a meeting.'

'There's really no need to talk about women like that,' Grafton heard himself explain sanctimoniously. 'That sort of language says a lot more about you than the girl you're taking out. It means you're afraid of women.'

Ken grunted on the phone.

'Why don't you fuck a dog instead?' asked Grafton half seriously.

There was no reply.

'Or an otter? Why don't you fuck an otter?'

'But they're nice little animals,' said Ken.

'Could you say that again?'

'I said . . .' faltered Ken. 'Well . . . what are you driving at?'

'That your response says something pretty powerful about your attitude to women. Like most alcoholics,' Grafton said with a laugh, 'your state of sexual maturation leaves something to be desired!'

Ken said he didn't understand, but that he'd think about it. Whatever happened, he felt sure he wouldn't drink.

Taking him into Ken's room, the bed exactly as he had left it, Mrs Laver showed Grafton a story Ken wrote when he was still at school. 'THE MASKED AVENGER – A THRILLER BY KENNETH A LAVER. FORM 4C', hand-written in a Dux exercise book with a hangdog photo of the author, minus a mask, pasted on the front.

'He was starting to do so *well*.' Still holding the exercise book, she looked up, moist rheumy eyes half closed. 'We haven't got Ken's note back yet.'

'There's going to be an inquest,' said thin Mr Laver,

90

rubbing his bald patch over and over again. 'It could be months.'

His Mum, bloated in her cotton dress, tried to pacify the black-and-white kelpie at her feet. 'Ken so wanted to stop drinking. But he had to take pills to get him to the meetings. He was so *frightened* of people.

'When he had to go into hospital for more treatment he didn't want a soul to know. If anyone rang we had to say he was staying with friends. I told him I thought the AA's wouldn't mind. But he said they would. I asked him, couldn't I just tell you, but Kenny wouldn't let me. You know how stubborn he is.' Her old arms flayed at the empty, unkempt bed.

'The police said that in his note he told us not to worry, and to ask you, that you'd understand.' She clutched Grafton by the arm. 'Do you?'

'Thank you for coming,' said Mr Laver, peeling hand lightly touching Grafton's shoulder. 'You know, we've been expecting it for ages. His psychiatrist, Dr Weisen, told Ken's mother three years ago that there wasn't any hope.'

Mrs Laver gave him a handful of home-grown chokos and custard apples.

'Do you think he's at peace now?'

The angry kelpie blocked the door. 'How are we going to look after Nipper?'

'If you can,' said Mr Laver, taking the dog in his arms, 'please come and see us again.'

'My sad lost friend,' Grafton cried, backing his off-white Honda onto the road, 'wherever you are, I hope to Christ there are otters.'

A Force in the Corridors

Grafton Everest had just been deported from America. On the plane, wondering what to do when he returned, he fixed upon an Idea. Grafton had no theological training (he hardly ever read the Bible), but he got it into his head that it would be an excellent idea to be teaching Biblical Studies. The more he thought about it, the more he felt convinced. Having recently joined Alcoholics Anonymous, but still taking tablets, Grafton was feeling very spiritual.

The day after he arrived, he rang the Victorian Education Department. Providentially, a Biblical Studies course was set on the secondary school curriculum: not religious instruction, but, in fact, Biblical Studies. Having a BA, Grafton had left the Department four times previously after brief money-making stints. It usually took about three months for that type of information to surface, by which time he would be gone again. The late '60s was a seller's market – teachers were in short supply. At his own request, Grafton was assigned to a school near his parents' house in South Caulfield. Having no money and a very thin grip on what others called reality, Grafton was conscripted into staying at home for the first time since he started university. The house was only ten minutes walk to Seaview High, a school which had never before had a Biblical Studies master. The prospect of a new career exhilarated him – Grafton felt that perhaps it augured well.

Word soon got around school that the Biblical Studies bloke was coming. The members of the male staff especially wondered what their new addition would look like.

Before his appointment with the principal at midday Wednesday, Grafton went to the TAB to bet on the daily double. With an outlay of $40, he took the field in the first leg, coupled four times with horses number 12 and 13. That was his system. Just before noon, Grafton strolled up to Seaview High, wearing an iridescent orange suit that he'd bought in a Cleveland ghetto sale, a purple jerkin, an Isadora Duncan scarf, riding boots, hair down to his back, sporting a great red beard. He weighed sixteen stone. Bombed out on a combination of amphetamines and barbiturates, Grafton had a copy of his father's Good Book under his arm. Thus he was intro-duced to Miss Owens, the female principal, and Mr Mould, senior subject master. A small polite woman wearing light red lipstick, the principal inquired what had drawn him to Biblical Studies. 'It's hard to explain,' he boomed, 'but I just knew that I had to teach it. I've never felt at home in the world,' he continued, looking at thin Mr Mould who stared blankly ahead. 'At best I seem like a visitor.

'You see,' he said, pointing to Miss Owen's desk and chair, 'this isn't ultimate reality. The world of space and time is an illusion. But the world of the spirit,' he sighed, holding out the Bible, 'the . . .'

'I understand,' Miss Owens interrupted gently and smiled. 'Coming here is obviously very important to you. Mr Mould will make you feel at home.'

After a perfunctory tour of inspection, the senior sub-ject master ushered Grafton into the male staff room. The seated men listened suspiciously as Grafton started his spiel. In the middle of it he asked, 'Would you mind if I listened to a race?' The men certainly didn't mind that. Asked what he'd backed in the first leg, Grafton answered, 'The Field.' He produced a wad of tickets.

Curiosity aroused, they duly listened to the broadcast at 2 o'clock. It was a mid-week race at Werribee. An outsider, Gold Belle, won at 33 to 1. In Melbourne, before the running of the second leg, they always announced what the daily double would pay. Gold Belle, coupled with horse number 12, a gelding called Exhibition, would have paid about $200, multiplied by four times. Number 13, The Gannet, a seven-year-old, would pay $450. In Grafton's case, multiplied by four. He explained that 12 and 13 were his lucky numbers. A majority of the men stayed back after school to listen to the race. Exhibition skipped to the lead but faded after five furlongs. A furlong from home, the favourite was cantering along in front looking a certainty to win, when out of the ruck like a lightning bolt came The Gannet. Number 13 won by a short half head, at 50 to 1. In front of the men, their new Biblical Studies master had just won close to two grand.

Those that believed in God thought that the Power had sent him, while others of more agnostic persuasion were intensely interested in what seemed more than mere good fortune. 'You are indeed welcome to the school,' Ashley Plunkitt, the pock-marked Sri Lankan, said formally. Impecunious, but very proud, he had been a game-keeper at Nandy before he came to Australia. 'Perhaps we can do business together,' he said, obviously speaking for the group. On the spot, a staff gambling syndicate was formed. The men, many of whom could ill-afford it, some with children and second mortgages, all put $100 in to start a direct telephone account with the TAB. Grafton was unanimously elected Tipster. The Treasurer was Ashley Plunkitt. As the Economics Master he was good at maths. The only member of the junior male staff who didn't join the syndicate was Rodney Skippen, a member of the Exclusive Brethren. He didn't join for religious reasons.

The School virtually came to a standstill. Instead of teaching Biblical Studies, Everest spent most of his time in the sick bay, by the telephone, betting on almost anything that moved – interstate trotters, greyhounds, and mid-week provincial meetings. An elaborate 'tic-tac' system was devised whereby the masters let each other know how the races, or whatever they were betting on, were going. When not actually forced to be in class, the men were either scrutinising The Sun's racing liftout or huddled over the radio listening to broadcasts. Instead of supervising yard duty at lunchtime and recess, the masters spent their time studying Form. The final choice was Grafton's, but they all had a say. Grafton eventually did not teach at all. The man who minded Biblical Studies was the Phys. Ed. master, Gordon Fields, known as Noddy because Gordon spelt backwards was Nodrog. An aggressive, energetic little man, who liked more than an occasional ale, Noddy would stand in front of classes and get Grafton's students – all from Forms 1 and 2 – to puzzle about Heriticus and Deuteronomy and the story of Nebuchadnezzar. Noddy, who had taken out two shares in the syndicate himself, never got beyond the Old Testament as he, along with all the junior men save Rodney Skippen, waited anxiously for results. Due to judicious place betting (mainly at the instigation of Ashley Plunkitt), the bank doubled in the first two months and the atmosphere along the corridors was extremely optimistic. The Good News continued – like the mills of God, slow, but extremely sure, as Ashley reminded them, drawing on his Baptist past. Tony McIntosh, the twice married art teacher, dreamt of buying a power boat, while other masters announced plans of extended holidays and early retirement.

At the syndicate's first meeting for October, held in the sick bay, Grafton announced that he'd had a dream. 'I heard a voice calling, "Think of the Lillies in the Field . . ." and I saw a bookmaker, weeping, with an empty bag, pointing to numbers 12 and 13, saying, "It couldn't happen, it just couldn't happen . . ." '

'It means something,' Noddy insisted as he read over the Form. 'Lillies? . . . Harry White!' he cried out, pointing at the list of final acceptors. 'Harry White is riding Not Again in the first leg in Geelong.' Noddy was bouncing up and down like an animated dwarf. 'And look what he's on in the second – The Gannet!'

'It must be a sign,' Grafton said. 'Let's put on all our

bank. Back them each to win and take the Daily Double as well.'

Ashley Plunkitt cautioned at throwing hard-earned money to the wind, while Tony McIntosh, attempting to impress, pointed out that Needs Must was in the second leg as well, and that name was decidedly Biblical too. 'No,' Grafton said, closing his eyes. 'It's Not Again and The Gannet. We'll put on the lot.' Prudent to the last, Ashley opted for quitting while he was well in front. His place in the syndicate was taken by Rodney Skippen – the Exclusive Brethren's only representative at Seaview High.

When Not Again won at tens, after surviving a protest, the sick room was electric. At 3.15 all members of the junior male staff, including Rodney Skippen who had forsaken his disciplinary forays into the playground, were hunched breathlessly in front of the wireless. Bert Bryant read out the quotes. The Gannet had been backed in to 7 to 2s. Still they'd win a fortune. Charlie Mould came in to see why the junior forms had been sent home and was firmly told to piss off. It was Cup week at Geelong.

The race began. Needs Must was left at the barrier and The Gannet took the lead. The male staff cheered and cheered. Mrs Richards, the tealady, was almost mobbed. 'Go on, you beauty. Ride him, Harry White. Go on, go on, garn The Gannet.' The Gannet held the lead and the oh-so-proud animal increased its margin, to one length, two lengths, three. The Gannet romped home a full five lengths in front of the field.

The men, holding hands, danced round and round the table on which Grafton sat crosslegged.

'It's a bloody *miracle*', cried Tony McIntosh whose mortgage had been paid off. Noddy was close to tears. 'I'm going to buy a pub and live in Yarram and never teach or exercise again.'

'You bewdy Grafton . . . Three cheers for the Bible, Hip, Hip, *Hooray*.'

At that Miss Owens came in, right arm held up for

96

silence; in her left hand was a departmental envelope, open.

'You've heard the Good News, boys,' she said sweetly 'Now we've got some bad – Grafton has to leave. Even though he's been quite a force in the corridors, the Department is absolutely adamant. He shouldn't have been employed in the first place.'

'Oh, no,' cried the junior men, as one. 'He was sent to us,' wailed Noddy.

'The Lord giveth, the Lord taketh away,' said the principal. 'One has to accept the things one cannot change. Isn't that right, Grafton?'

Grafton nodded his assent. 'Anyway, the boy needs a rest,' the principal said firmly, gathering the junior men around her. 'There is a time for every purpose under heaven. Now Grafton has to go.' The masters turned sadly to walk away. It didn't seem fair. 'Don't worry about me,' said Grafton brightly, 'the Lord does move in mysterious ways.'

'His wonders to perform,' added Molly Owens. She took Grafton aside and whispered, 'Give up those tablets. And stick with the AAs ... They fixed *me* up,' she added loudly, with a twinkle in her eye.

'So go on home, boys, and spend up big. Tuesday's Cup Day.'

At the farewell party, Noddy proposed a toast, in lemonade: 'May The Gannet strike again.' Although Grafton moved on to greener pastures, The Gannet never did.

IV

Before you can get your finger out of your
arse, you're asleep.
>   *Lennie Bruce, Seconal commercial*

Grafton Has a Holiday

Six months had passed since Grafton had attempted to relax. The trip to Malacca had temporarily rejuvenated him, although mouth ulcers and the recurrent pain in his left side had put him into a black humour for much of the time. As the past receded, Grafton turned everything into fiction. From his current perspective the trip had been an outstanding success. So much so that the word 'Malacca' was now a symbol for all that was good in an essentially bleak world.

Back in Brisbane, Grafton was feeling even more strung out than usual – his overeating was getting worse and he couldn't write a word. All his illnesses had returned. Overcome with helplessness, Grafton realised that another half of his life lay ahead. Appalled, his nerves kept signalling messages of doom – 'I can't last. I just can't last without a holiday.' During a lengthy argument over tea about Janet's remodelling the house, which disturbed his sleep, Grafton fastened onto the idea that they should go away again.

'Don't forget that you take yourself with you,' Janet said sweetly. 'And that you bring yourself back as well.'

'All my friends travel and do things,' he whinged ignoring that in reality Janet was his only friend. 'I never get to go *anywhere*,' Grafton harped, banging the laden bed-tray with his fist. He had bought the tray, made of cane, for their second anniversary. 'Well, my love, if you think we can afford it, and you don't blame

101

me if anything goes wrong, we'll go wherever you want.' 'Really,' said Grafton, moving forward to adjust his pyjama top and demolishing a second helping of lemon chicken. His eyes lit up at the prospect of getting his own way.

In an unaccustomed rush of largesse, Grafton wiped his chin with his hand and asked, 'Then where would you like to go? It's only fair you have a say.'

'If you really want to know, my love,' replied Janet, passing him a mango, 'I'd like to go to Bali.' Her winsome face looked wistful and far away. 'I feel in tune whenever I go there. Part of the natural order of things. Bali is my spiritual home,' she sighed.

'Bali it is then,' announced Grafton. 'I'll organise it.'

'Whatever you say, my love,' said Janet, who went downstairs to her loom.

Nigel had dealt with him before. Grafton could see his sad, lacklustre face talking close to the telephone. 'That doesn't seem possible, Doctor,' Nigel said patiently. It was the fifth time Grafton had rung that day. 'One can't include Singapore and Bali on the one excursion fare.' 'Why not?' growled Grafton. 'Well, as I have tried to explain, Doctor, the passage is based on the number of airmiles, and Brisbane, Sydney, Singapore, Bali, Brisbane, Sydney exceeds the maximum.' 'Well, see what you can do,' persisted Grafton unhearing. 'I'll make it worth your while,' he added, quite untruthfully.

'Now, about accommodation,' he continued. 'My wife has heard good reports about the Tjuamphuan in Ubud. I'd like to spend our whole two weeks there.'

'I'm afraid I couldn't recommend that, Doctor. It's only local Indonesian food, there aren't proper toilets and there's no air-conditioning.'

'I can't stand air-conditioning,' screamed Grafton. 'How many times do I have to tell you that?' Nigel's head crowded over with too many inputs of contradictory information. 'I'm in the wrong game,' thought Nigel, who had six children. Nigel hated going away on

overseas trips – one of the prime perks for Travel
Agents. In fact he abhorred travel. 'My wife *likes* natural surroundings. She's a weaver,' Grafton explained.
'The Doctor's wife is a bit of an artist,' Grafton overheard Nigel say away from the telephone. 'So we'll
book them both in for the lot – all meals, one full-day
car trip and two half days . . . That'll be fine, Doctor, at
least we've fixed up your accommodation.'

'But still keep trying about Singapore, okay. I'll ring
again tomorrow,' said Grafton. To Nigel it sounded omi-
nously like a threat.

'Indonesian,' Janet explained, 'is the simplest language in the world.' Assured that even cretins can
learn it, Grafton decided that he would embark on
acquiring a skill. 'Speaking another language involves
actually *thinking* another way,' he explained to Che,
the Burmese. If there was one thing Grafton could do
with right now it was a new way of thinking. 'Good
Thinking leads to Good Acting,' he crooned to the cat
who unsuccessfully tried to get away. Grafton's
attempt at learning Russian, in Perth, had been an out-
and-out failure. Bahasa Indonesia in Brisbane sounded
much more like his cup of tea.

'Why don't you borrow my English-Indonesian
phrase book, my love,' asked Janet. 'It might be an
interest before we leave.'

'One must do things properly,' said Grafton, finishing
off a piece of chocolate cake. He consulted his diary
and rang the University. 'Hello, this is Dr Everest. I
won't be in today. Could you please connect me with
the Language Centre?'

Trudi Krausman outlined the choices. In the end
Grafton took the new language tape course, plus a
book. He had the eighteen tapes sent out by courier.
They were due to depart in twenty-one days. 'I'll play
each tape four times a day, and leave myself three days
for refreshers. By the time I arrive in Bali, I'll speak the
language like a native. Of course, the real natives
speak Balinese,' Grafton explained unnecessarily to

103

the cat. 'But that won't worry us, will it?' Che sat silently, just out of reach.

Grafton waited until Janet went out shopping before he turned on the cassette downstairs. He confidently repeated the first phrase, 'Selamat pagi – Good morning.' In fact it was the afternoon. 'Ini – This,' said the tape. 'Ini,' repeated Grafton. 'Ini medja – This is a table.' 'Itu – That,' 'Itu,' chorused Grafton. 'Itu kursi – That is a chair,' 'Itu kursi,' boomed Grafton, pointing.

The first five minutes went well. 'Hari – Day.' 'Hari-hari – every day,'' Hari-hari,' Grafton said with a smile. 'Bagus – Good.' 'Bagoos,' Grafton emphasised, stroking the reluctant Burmese.

'In Bahasa Indonesia, there is no verb "to be" ', warned the tape. 'The adjective generally follows the noun.' 'What is an adjective?' Grafton asked out loud. 'Adjectives, prepositions, pronouns, nouns.' Despite his three degrees, Grafton had never managed to fathom grammar at school. Consequently he had no idea what was meant.

Oblivious, the tape wheezed on. 'Ada lapan puluh orang laki-laki – There are eighty men.' Before Grafton could get to laki-laki the man's reedy voice said 'Apa tiga orang perempuan itu makan – What are those three women eating?' 'Apa tiger,' growled Grafton. 'Fuck the women eating,' he cried in anguish. 'It's all happening too fast. I can't keep up.'

'Saya ada tiga orang anak,' bawled the tape. 'Saja belum pandai bahasa Indonesia. Kalau kurang betul tolong betukan.' It continued unperturbed. Apart from 'bahasa Indonesia' the words were totally incomprehensible. Grafton snapped off the machine and hurled the tape at the cat. 'Perhaps I really do have brain damage,' he whimpered. 'And I thought it was going to be easy.' Grafton took Che upstairs and angrily ate another piece of cake.

'I won't have you listening to the tape at home,' he screamed at Janet, who seemed to be learning the language with no pain at all. 'It makes me feel inadequate. So turn the tape *off*.'

'I don't think that's fair, darling. In fact I think it's cruel.' 'Life's cruel,' retorted Grafton. 'At least it is to me. I don't want to go,' he said petulantly. 'Go where?' inquired Janet. 'To Bali,' Grafton snapped. 'Well then we won't, my love.' 'Of course we'll go,' thundered Grafton. 'Why do you have to be so agreeable?' he fumed. 'I'm sorry, my love,' said Janet, backing out of the room to finish her work downstairs.

'Could I speak to Nigel?'

'I'm sorry Mr Ritchie's no longer with us'.

'What a pity,' said Grafton. 'He really was most helpful.' 'My name is Helen Fondes, Nigel's replacement. Can I help?'

'Indeed you can,' replied Grafton, quickly coming to life.

After going through the whole procedure of Singapore and Bali once again, Grafton inquired about injections. 'Cholera, smallpox. And it's most advisable to take malaria tablets. Bali is a high risk area, especially in December, the rainy season. It's the effect of pesticides,' explained Helen. 'Aerial spraying has produced a highly resistant form. Up to fifteen years ago malaria had been wiped out in New Guinea, but now it's more virulent than before. By the way,' said Helen, pausing for breath, 'your return flights are confirmed. You're flying Garuda both ways.'

'Hello, Doctor,' inquired Mr Oldfield, the chemist. 'How are you today?' 'Only fair,' said Grafton, eyeing off the coloured condoms that were displayed on the front counter. His eyes fixed on Hawaiian Delight – orange ones with tendril-like ticklers at the end. Tall, pale and predatory, Mac Oldfield was the most politically involved of all the local shopkeepers. Much of Mac's time was spent posting up 'Zero Income Tax' posters and talking on talkback radio. Minimal Government and No Universities were two of his ideological pillars. As Grafton waited for his prescriptions to be filled, the topic was the Federal Government's purchase of a luxury aircraft. 'If I bought a five million dollar aircraft,' explained Mr Oldfield, poking his head out of the dispensing hatch, 'my business would go bankrupt overnight.' Grafton stifled a momentary desire to explain that a pharmacist wouldn't be likely to buy an aircraft, but instead agreed and asked for some Digesic, without a prescription. 'My arthritis is playing up. And you'd better give me some malaria tablets.'

'Off again are we?' winked Mr Oldfield. 'Another research trip?'

'No I'm paying for it myself. Any side effects with these malaria tablets?'

'Only one in a million, Doctor. You'll be right as rain.'

Holiday Magic caught Grafton's eyes – they were iridescent green with three gigantic spikes on the end. 'I'll have a box of those too,' said Grafton looking Mr Oldfield straight in the eye. 'I'll give Janet a surprise in Bali.'

'Bali is it Doctor? You're certainly in a hard game,' continued Mr Oldfield, who didn't bat an eye. 'No need to wrap them, Doctor? Never know when you'll need them.'

Mr Oldfield slapped him on the back and gave him a car-sticker. 'When you're next speaking on the box you might give the cause a plug, okay?'

Grafton was trying on a Holiday Magic when the phone rang. It was only half on; all three spikes pointed to the ground.

'Hello, Doctor, it's Helen Fondes from National Bank Travel. I'm afraid there's been a change of plans.'

'A change of what?' boomed Grafton.

'Unfortunately, one of Garuda's planes crashed and they've cancelled your Bali flight to bring back a bunch of pilgrims from Mecca.'

'How *dare* you,' screamed Grafton. 'How dare you change our plans. This is the most *incompetent* travel agency I've *ever* dealt with.'

106

'I'm sorry, Doctor, but it's not really our fault.'

'Of course it's your fault,' screamed Grafton.

'I can get you on a Qantas flight – only one day earlier.'

'That's no good,' cried Grafton. 'All our plans will have to be changed. I can't *stand* change,' he screamed. 'I can't cope. I'd arranged to see my publisher,' whimpered Grafton, forgetting that he hadn't written a line for months. 'And now my book will be delayed . . . what's that, you stupid girl?' Helen Fondes was crying, tears gushed uncontrollably. 'Please don't cry,' begged Grafton. The sobs continued unabated. 'Oh, please forgive me,' Grafton implored. 'I haven't been feeling well,' he said. 'I've got a sore throat and my pain's come back. I find going on holidays very difficult. I know it wasn't your fault. Yes, of course, I'll go on the Qantas flight. No, you've been very helpful. I'll just have to ring Sydney, that's all. Now, please stop crying.' Helen did, and reassured again, hung up.

'Thank Christ for that.' Grafton was exhausted. He hung his head in his hands and wept.

'My God, what's the matter?' shrieked Janet.

'Our bloody trip's been changed.'

'No!' said Janet. 'What's that thing between your legs?'

'Oh, just a surprise for Bali,' he said snapping off the Holiday Magic and sitting in a corner crossly, by himself. 'What a strange thing,' said Janet.

'I'm sick to death of this bloody holiday,' he whinged, blaming Janet.

'But darling,' Janet said stroking his arm, 'it wasn't my idea. It really wasn't. Now, tell me what the trouble is,' she coaxed, dropping the condom into the rubbish bin. 'I'm sure we'll be able to work it out. Why don't you get to bed,' she said brightly, 'and let me get you something to eat.'

'Now it looks like there's going to be an air-strike,' exclaimed Grafton. He threw the newspaper to the end of the bed. 'With our luck we'll be trapped in Sydney for weeks and we won't be able to get in or out.'

'Things have worked out up to now,' comforted Janet, bringing him the breakfast tray which fitted snugly over his thighs. She propped up his pillows. 'If you just let go and trust, everything will turn out fine.'

'Why does this *always* happen to me?' said Grafton, stuffing in a cheese omelette. 'The baggage porters *and* the refuellers are likely to go out. They're holding this bloody country to *ransom*,' Grafton screamed. 'Just because some lazy buggers want a forty six dollar a week increase. Forty six dollars! Can you imagine?' Janet shook her head. 'I can't go on on like this,' he lamented. 'It takes so much energy just surviving. If I can't cope here, how will I ever manage in Bali?' He accentuated 'Bali' with a baring of his teeth. 'I've got that pain in my left side, mouth ulcers from the injections, and I can't sit still long enough to write a note to the milkman.'

'Just now, my love, you're not *supposed* to write. You've had a hard year, that's why we're going on holidays.'

'But it looks like we won't be able to go,' he whined. 'I'm going to call it off,' screamed Grafton. 'I can't bear this insecurity.'

'Why don't we keep our options open?' suggested Janet. 'If you can just learn to let go, everything will be alright. Now, let's take our malaria tablets, two this Friday before we go and make sure we take them while we're away.'

'Those pills taste *dreadful*,' Grafton gasped, dialling. 'Hello, could I speak to Helen Fondes please? This is Doctor Everest.'

Grafton was jumping from one foot to the other. The taxi was ten minutes late. 'Are you sure Che will be alright at home?' Grafton asked for the fifth time. 'She's such a little pussy.'

'I'm sure Susan will take good care of her,' said

Janet. 'It's only next door and she'll shut the pussy door at night.'

'It's so unfair. Taxis are *always* late and we still don't know if the overseas flights are on.'

'I don't think you'll need that jumper, dear. Bali is very warm.'

'I'm sensitive to the cold,' Grafton snapped. 'And what about Sydney – it's like the Antarctic.'

'Not in December, love.'

'Here it comes,' flapped Grafton as he bundled the suitcases outside. 'Are you sure we've got enough clothes?'

The taxidriver was a prophet of doom. 'There's no chance of getting out of Sydney. No chance. If I was you I'd stay in Brisbane.'

'If I were *you*,' Grafton moralised to the driver, 'I'd concentrate on getting to people's places on time. Now it looks like we're going to be late.'

Sitting in the front of the cab, Grafton wheeled around to Janet. 'Have you got our tickets? Christ, this is a nightmare.' Grafton almost sobbed. 'I wish I'd never left home . . .

'I *hate* flying in the back of planes and I hate sitting in "Smoking". That's why I vomited on the way down,' he said. 'We've had to wait an hour for our luggage and now I've got the going away pain in my left side. I hope it's all worthwhile,' lamented Grafton to the air.

'One or two days in Bali and you'll be right as rain,' cheered Janet. 'Mark my words.'

'I hope the monsoons don't come while we're there,' he replied.

As they jostled through the crowd to catch the transit bus to get to the international terminus, Grafton angrily announced, 'I feel like death at the feast – my stomach's on fire, my sinuses are blocked and I've still got that terrible pain in my left side. Do I look alright?' he asked.

'You look fine, my love. You'll be alright,' she said taking him by the hand.

'But look at all those people,' Grafton groaned as they edged up to the departure lounge. 'It's absolute chaos.'

'I just want to be on my own and go to bed.'

'I beg your pardon?' said the ticket allocator.

'My name is Doctor Everest,' said Grafton, pulling himself together. 'I must have a non-smoking window seat in the middle of the plane. I don't feel well,' Grafton explained.

'Is the flight to Bali going?' asked Janet.

'Qantas is,' said the girl, 'but Garuda is grounded.'

'I told you that the girl from the travel agent was doing a good job,' Janet enthused. 'Everything is working out fine.'

'Welcome aboard your Qantastic Funjet,' beamed the chief steward. All the stewards, wearing floral shirts, looked like ageing hipsters. The hostesses, heavily rouged and with bright red lipstick, had flowers pinned on their uniforms above a brown plastic boomerang. As the passengers climbed aboard, a motif of hibiscus circling the inside of the 727 came into view. 'Hello, I'm Doctor Everest,' said Grafton, royally reaching out his hand. The other passengers were kept waiting in a queue behind. 'I'm a friend of Judge Jim Cleaver. He said to make contact.' Janet winced as Grafton used his influence, which he had promised not to do. 'Good for you, Doctor,' said Noel Jones, the chief steward. 'A friend of the Judge, eh? I wish he was judging our wage case right now.' Noel personally showed them to their seats by the window. 'We'll have a surprise for you later,' hinted the steward. 'I don't drink,' said Grafton severely. Noel laughed out loud and wheeled away.'At least we've got a window seat,' Grafton grumped. 'Perhaps they'll let us in first class.' In fact, it was a one-class jet.

'Isn't it exciting?' said Janet, holding his hand.

'I hope my ears don't block up,' said Grafton, puffing on his inhaler and taking some barley sugar. He pressed the call button. 'What's the film?' asked

110

Grafton. 'There is no film,' the plump steward explained.

'What a pity. Do you have a book then? And a glass of milk?'

Grafton selected a spy book. As always he couldn't follow the plot. 'You know,' said Grafton, as Janet gazed contentedly out the window. 'Travel agents could easily be couriers . . . and smuggle in information or drugs in packages.' 'Don't be silly,' Janet said warmly. 'Who would want to smuggle drugs *into* Bali? They don't need drugs,' she exclaimed brightly. 'They're very spiritual people.'

'I wish he hadn't taken us into the cockpit,' complained Grafton. 'It doesn't look safe and it's so small.'

'It's Funtastic Game Time,' Noel Jones' nasal voice boomed over the amplifier. The steward and hostesses distributed a map of Bali, covered with numbers, beside each place name to every passenger, and a Funtastic Card with six numbers. 'How do you play this bloody game?' Grafton grumbled to the blond-haired steward who had brought him his milk.

'Well, you tick off each number on the card that corresponds to the numbers, on the map of Bali,' the steward explained nonchalantly. 'See 41,' he pointed to 41 on the card. Grafton quickly crossed off his numbers. 'Does *everyone* win this silly game?'

'I haven't,' said Janet sadly. 'There's no number 8 on mine.' Suddenly a dawn of realisation flashed. 'You mean I've *won*?' The junior steward smiled. 'I wish I could pick horses like that, Doctor!' He nudged Grafton and went up front. 'The winner of a dinner for two *and* a Cultural Night,' Noel's voice crooned, 'at the Bali Hyatt, is seat number 67'. Sporadic clapping burst out. 'Its been a fix,' Grafton whispered, leaning over Janet.

'Be quiet, darling,' she said calmly. 'It wasn't your fault.'

'How dare they,' Grafton said, but the idea of announcing to the plane that the game had been rigged seemed fraught with difficulties. 'That spoilt my flight,' moralised Grafton as the aircraft taxied in to Denpassar. 'I feel so guilty.'

'Tell the Judge we took care of you, Doctor,' beamed Noel farewelling them at the door. 'A fella never knows when you'll be operating on him, does he? See ya doc,' said the chief steward slapping him on the back. 'And welcome to Bali – it's *Fan Tastic*.'

The evening rain had stopped as Oka, the Tjuamphuan's driver drove them to the hotel. 'My name is Satoya,' beamed the jaunty man in front. 'You don't mind if I ride, I hope?' he said for the third time. Grafton crossly shook his head. He often got carsick in the back, but Janet had asked him this once to ride in the back with her. Sick looking young western girls and trendy tourists wearing sarongs whizzed by as they passed Kuta village on the way in to Denpassar. 'It seems so much more commercial,' Janet said sadly. 'But Ubud will still be wonderful, just you wait and see.'

'There is only *one* doctor in Ubud,' smiled Mr Satoya. 'I would much like for you to meet him.'

'I'm not a medical doctor. I'm a doctor in phil-os-ophy,' replied Grafton in the slow, loud way he used when speaking to foreigners.

'I know,' said Mr Satoya. 'Very sorry. P.H.D. I too am a teacher. I have been to *Darwin*,' he said with pride. 'On an exchange programme.'

'How did you like it?' Janet asked.

'Don't encourage him,' whispered Grafton. 'He's getting on my nerves.'

'Very good, very good,' said Mr Satoya in his polite, but persistent way. 'Darwin itself was *paradise*,' Mr Satoya obviously meant what he said. 'Many steaks, many supermarkets, but some boys and girls were naughty. Other teachers come and help me,' he said. 'Very nice.'

'Mr Satoya,' announced Oka, the driver, in very deliberate English. 'Is teacher at Ubud.'

'Oh, good,' said Janet.

'He owns taxi,' said Oka, encouraged. 'And he helps me with English.'

'Good,' said Grafton in a very final way. 'We're going too *fast*,' demanded Grafton. 'I can't see a thing.'

'Very sorry,' said Oka, who slowed the taxi down.

'In Ubud school,' Mr Satoya said unperturbed, 'we have no naughty children – all bad ones, all lazy ones, all silly ones, send away. You see,' he said, 'many, many children want to come to school but very few places.' Mr Satoya, it eventuated, taught from eight until one, there being two lots of classes in the school. 'But often I go home at eleven,' he said warmly.

'And often he say today a holiday,' said Oka. Everyone in the taxi, except fat Grafton, laughed and laughed.

It was almost dark as they dropped Mr Satoya off at Peliaton, the dance village, on the outskirts of Ubud. 'Very pleased to meet you, Grafton, Janet,' said Mr Satoya, clasping his hands low. 'I hope you will come for tea at my house. After you see the Barong dance. Oka will let you know.'

'What a nice man,' said Janet. 'I would so much like to go.'

'We shall,' said Grafton, putting his arm around his wife. 'After all, it's a holiday.'

'This is the Tjuamphuan,' said Oka, proudly gesturing into the darkness. 'I hope you enjoy your stay. I your driver,' he said. 'You let your boy know and I come for you. I take you on *many* drives.'

Satra, their boy, a handsome white-teethed youth who looked only fifteen, opened the door and holding a kerosene lamp, bade them follow down a rocky path.

'We sign book tomorrow,' he said as he showed them to their bungalow. 'Now you have your free Welcome Drink,' he said, bowing low, 'and eat.'

'I don't drink,' said Grafton severely.

Satra smiling, did not comprehend.

'I don't drink al-co-hol,' said Grafton, very deliberately.

'Talking slowly doesn't really help, my love,' Janet leaned forward and said in Bahasa Indonesia, 'My husband cannot drink alcohol.'

'Welcome Drink only ricewine,' said Satra in English, his young eyes sparkling. He liked Janet already. Satra explained, 'Ricewine only *little* alcoholic.'

'It does not matter,' Grafton looked very nervous.

'My husband does not drink alcohol at all, understand, not *any*.'

'Not any,' repeated Satra, shaking his head. 'Very well,' he said to Grafton, his eyes lighting up, 'I will bring you fresh orange esdjeruk and for Janet Ricewine, yes?' 'Oh, yes, Terima Kasih,' said Janet, also bowing low. 'Thank you very much,' she explained to Grafton. 'Isn't this lovely,' said Janet, exploring the top floor of their thatched bungalow.

'No electric light, no taps, no noise and no telephone. We're going to have a wonderful holiday.' 'I'm hungry,' said Grafton finishing off his esdjeruk. 'That tasted good, I think I'll have another.'

'What a restful night's sleep I had,' said Janet snuggling up to him. 'Look how beautiful this is.' The curtain of last night's darkness had lifted. She pointed down to the trees, the ravine, the waterfall and the superbly tiered swimming pool. 'Sir Walter Spies designed that. That's his original bungalow,' she said gesturing to the grand structure up the hill. 'Margaret Mead stayed there,' she said deferentially. Margaret Mead was Janet's great hero. 'And to think we're here, together. Aren't we lucky?' she exclaimed, throwing her long and supple arms around him. 'To have each other, and to be so in love.' 'A fortunate man is a man who thinks he's fortunate,' announced Grafton, putting on his shorts. 'My word, that rice and mango supper was good,' he said, smacking his lips. 'Let's go down and get breakfast. I'm famished.'

Grafton vigorously beat the gong and told Satra they'd have the lot and an esdjeruk as well.

'Look at those flowers,' Janet enthused, pointing to

114

the arrangement of frangipanis on their carved wooden table, and to the yellow hibiscus flowers that had been picked and carefully placed in the vines that ran along their verandah. 'Isn't that a wonderful idea?'

Grafton grunted his assent as he ritually read his *Just for Today* book. It talked, as it often did, about gratitude and letting-go.

'I really should feel grateful,' said Grafton, reluctantly, as he and Janet sat in their cane chairs, beside their bungalow, overlooking the river in which boys and girls bathed naked and enthusiastically below.

'You'll get to feel close to the Power here, my love,' sighed Janet contentedly, 'I promise you that.'

'I must say it's pleasant enough,' said Grafton. 'It's totally different to what I imagined.'

'Well, my love,' explained Janet, 'nothing . . . nothing could be more different from urban Australia than the Balinese in these wonderful mountains. They've got a totally different sense of life and death, and of time too.'

'I hope Satra smartens up with my breakfast,' said Grafton, momentarily reminded. 'What's the word for quickly here?'

'Lekas, my love, but give the boy a chance.'

'There's a snake,' cried Grafton, leaping out of his chair and pointing at the vines below. 'It's a snake, a snake.' Grafton danced about wildly. 'There it goes.'

'Don't be silly,' purred Janet.

'It is a snake,' pleaded Grafton. 'A long thin snake on the vine. It is. It is.'

Satra arrived with his heavily laden tray. 'Oh, yes,' he said brightly. 'That a tree snake. It no hurt. Hurt snake is green.'

'The *green* snake is the dangerous one,' said Grafton slowly. 'That's right, only the green snake?'

'Only the green snake,' laughed Satra. 'You have your breakfast, okay?'

As they munched on banana and papaya and cheese omelettes, and thick black coffee and wads of toast and jam, Grafton watched his tree snake slither along the vines and the black ants running to and fro.

Satra stood silently near by.

'You want something?' asked Grafton.

'What is your programme for today?'

'What programme?' snapped Grafton.

'I think he wants us to tell him what we want to do,' Janet offered.

'You want go to Legong Dance? Go to Klungkung, buy antiques, go to Mas buy wood-carvings?' smiled Satra, adjusting his sarong.

'Oh, no,' said Grafton. 'We'll only have a little walk and rest today. We've just arrived.' Janet looked a trifle disappointed.

'One cannot experiment with one's health,' lectured Grafton. 'One has got to take things easy. Perhaps tomorrow,' he said to Satra, who turned to leave. 'But I'll have a Balinese massage at four.'

'Don't those frangipanis smell lovely?' Janet enthused.

'I hope no one uses the next bungalow. My big fear is that just as we're settled, hordes of people will descend on the Tjuamphuan. It's nearly Christmas.'

'I think the air strike will take care of that. Don't worry, my love.' As it was, the Tjuamphuan was almost deserted.

After a second cup of coffee, he and Janet, both dressed in white shorts and immense straw sunhats and armed with Janet's Instamatic, went for a languid walk across the long wooden bridge into Ubud village. They saw the King's Palace and the Museum, but best of all, they found a secluded local temple, across the river, that overlooked the Tjuamphuan.

'Look, there's our bungalow,' said Janet. 'Isn't it grand?'

After Janet had bargained for some batik, without buying any, they arrived home hot and very sticky.

'It's so oppressive,' whinged Grafton. 'It's worse than Brisbane,' he wheezed as he lay down on the bed. 'And my throat is sore,' he complained. 'I feel miserable.'

'You'll feel better when you've had some lunch,' she assured him. 'It's only ten minutes till the gong.'

The grass roofed restaurant overlooked a ravine. Grafton, who noticed to his pleasure that there were more staff than guests, selected a large unoccupied table. Each table was decorated with an arrangement of fresh flowers. Red hibiscus were placed equidistant around the whitewashed walls. A small gamelan orchestra played unobtrusively; the aroma of food, heaped on a serving table for all to see, wafted enticingly by. 'Look at the colours of the food,' said Janet. 'The Tjuamphuan has one of the best restaurants in Bali. I think this is the best place in the world.' Janet clapped her hands.

After grace, they tucked gustily into the chicken and rice and pork and rambutan sauce, and local vegetables. Grafton munched appreciatively and gave Janet and himself a large second helping.

'You don't mind if I sit down?' announced an athletic-looking man, sitting down without waiting for a reply. The head accompanying the voice looked almost the same as Grafton's except that it was thinner, slightly younger and wore no glasses. But the resemblance was uncanny.

'Mine's Michael Tutson. What's yours?' he said, proffering a hand. Grafton answered warily.

'Nice place? Cricket started? What's the score?' asked Michael. Questions ran out of his mouth like machine-gun bullets. Grafton felt as though he was being interrogated by himself.

'What score?' he mumbled testily.

'The cricket, billygoat?' said Michael laughing.

'Which cricket?' quizzed Grafton.

'The real cricket,' Michael retorted.

'Oh, the Test,' said Grafton, playing it dumb. He was pleased to see that their visitor, however unwelcome, was not commercial. 'Hughes scored a hundred,' said Grafton. 'But England won the test.'

'Good,' said Michael. 'That means I've won a hundred myself.'

Michael was a director in the Australian Opera Company – the youngest they'd ever had. He liked his work and he was not gay.

'I thought everyone was, in the opera.'

'All except me and most of the women,' laughed Michael. 'Fortunately,' he roared like a lion, reaching for a drink.

'Here comes the black rice pudding,' cried Janet with delight. 'It's my favourite dessert.'

'What's that you're reading?' Grafton asked.

'*A Man Called Intrepid*,' Michael answered. 'It's about Sir William Stephenson. The real man in charge of British spies during World War II.'

'You like spy stories?' inquired Grafton. 'So do I,' he said without waiting for an answer. 'You know I've often thought of being a spy.'

On and on they chatted after Janet had left to have an after luncheon nap.

'I really like cricket a lot,' Grafton said. 'I just pretended not to know. Cricket and spy stories are my two greatest loves.'

'Same with me,' said Michael. 'I hope I'll see you at dinner. I've got to learn a score. Opera,' he explained.

'I hope I'll see you,' replied Grafton warmly. He walked back happily to his bungalow. Grafton had made a friend.

'I think I like it here,' Grafton announced as he came upstairs.

'Do you, my love?' cried Janet. She was waiting for him, naked, eager. 'I was hoping you would.'

'I think I do,' said Grafton earnestly, taking off his pants. 'I think I really do.'

At six-thirty on the dot, they were back for dinner. Dutch-Indonesian kerosene lamps hung above the large wooden tables; outside fireflies danced. While Grafton had an esdjeruk and Janet and Michael drank rice wine, Michael told them all about opera.

118

'We'll go when you come to Brisbane,' Grafton announced. 'I've only ever seen one opera before – about convicts – it was terribly boring.'

'Mind if I join you?' said an aggressively American voice belonging to a close-cropped middle-aged female. Conspicuously placing a copy of *The Women's Room* on the table, the American sat down.

'You don't mind if I smoke?' she announced, lighting up.

'Actually, I do,' said Grafton firmly. 'I do mind,' he said to emphasise the point. 'I'm an asthmatic.'

'Well then,' said the woman, unbelieving. 'I'll just blow the smoke the other way.'

'No, you won't,' said Michael, 'I detest people smoking while I eat.'

'So do I,' chimed in Janet, having a large swig of her rice wine.

'Well, I guess I'm not welcome,' pouted the woman, who hadn't had time to volunteer her name.

'Not at the dinner table,' said Grafton. 'Actually, smokers aren't welcome, period. No offence,' he said brightly. 'But in any case, we prefer to eat alone.'

The feminist angrily picked up her pack and left.

'Good for you,' said Michael.

'Good for you,' said Grafton. 'It's a filthy habit. I used to smoke sixty a day.'

'So did I,' said Michael.

'Good on us all,' said Janet.

'I went five times to the Seventh Day Adventist Five-Day Plan and twice to a hypnotherapist. Will-power alone doesn't work with me.'

'What did?' said Michael.

'I did,' exclaimed Janet brightly. 'Payment by results,' he explained. 'And the day-at-a-time technique. I don't smoke for just today.'

The three munched happily through a large and enjoyable Indonesian meal, followed by a mango for dessert, and many cups of black coffee.

'Don't I know you?' inquired a voice from an adjoining table.

'Good God, it's Grafton Everest,' she said, answering herself. 'I thought you were dead.'

'How do you know her?' Janet mouthed softly.

'I think she was a student of mine, in Perth,' answered Grafton, slightly abashed. He took Janet's hand. 'It was a *long* time ago.'

'You sly old fox,' whispered Michael.

'Don't you remember?' persisted the girl, clad in denim. She was wearing an orange headband. 'The name's Amanda.'

'Vaguely,' said Grafton. 'A lot of the past is a blackout.'

'It must be ten years ago,' said Amanda. 'Something *good* has happened to you,' she enthused, laughing loudly.

'I don't drink,' said Grafton severely.

'This is my husband, Victor. We're off to Kintamani tomorrow.' Grafton noticed he had a glass eye.

'Mind if we join you?'

'You don't smoke, do you?' asked Michael brightly. Janet giggled.

'Only dope,' said the petite Amanda.

'I don't approve of dope,' explained Grafton.

'I'm not smoking now,' said the girl.

'And I've never smoked,' said her husband.

'Well you're as welcome as the flowers in May,' said Janet, reaching out her hand, 'I don't think we've met.'

After introductions, they talked long into the night, drinking whiskey and rice wine, with fresh orange juice and lime cordial for Grafton. Amanda was now a speech therapist, her husband a psychiatrist. It was their first time in Bali.

'There's very little mental illness among the Balinese,' Janet explained. 'Except for those who run amok.'

'Amok! Amok!' cried Michael, who ran in and out of

the Tjuamphuan tables, much to the delight of the boys and stern-faced Oka II who ran the bar. They discussed the wonders of Bali late into the night.

Being a full moon, they all went for a swim, except Grafton, who didn't want to risk catching a cold. Then they came back to the restaurant. As they talked into the early morning, the frogs choired on, encouraged by the moon.

'What a wonderful night,' said Janet, blowing out the bed-lamp. 'Listen to the ghekkos.'

'You know, I can communicate sober,' said Grafton thoughtfully.

'We've never been so long with strangers,' said Janet, 'and so at ease.'

'And I never felt sick at all,' said Grafton.

'I told you you'd relax in Bali, my love.'

'I don't even feel tired,' Grafton said.

'That's lucky,' said Janet slyly, and snuggled up close.

'Experience of time is very strange here,' philosophised Grafton. 'It seems to go so slow, yet it's not at all unpleasant.'

'Not at all, my love.' Janet took off his glasses and kissed him firmly on the mouth. Grafton reached for the Holiday Magic.

At 4 p.m. Mr Satoya and Oka arrived with two motor bikes. Grafton nervously sat behind the school teacher as they drove through Ubud.

'After we see cock fights,' said Mr Satoya, 'I will take you to see my resting place.'

Almost a hundred men gathered in a circle exchanging bets while the owners strapped knives onto the legs of the cocks. Grafton was terrified one of the cocks would fly out of the circle slashing him with its blade. 'The man strokes his cock to make it big and strong,' said Mr Satoya straight-faced. Grafton was increasingly frightened as the crowd's roar indicated the fight was about to begin.

'Loser loses all money and cock. Winner eats his cock,' Mr Satoya explained.

Janet watched with interest, but Grafton looked away to avoid being gashed in the eye by a wayward bird. Fortunately, the fight was a considerable anticlimax; the outsider lay down and refused to fight.

'Why are there walls around the compounds?' asked Grafton.

'The walls are to keep out evil spirits. And so are the dogs,' said Mr Satoya with a smile.

'What about bad dogs?' asked Grafton.

'There are no bad dogs in Bali,' said Mr Satoya.

'Then why does that dog have his tail cut off?'

'It tells the people it is not a good dog. It kills the ducks.'

'So its tail does not grow again like a tree?' said Grafton.

'Oh, ho, very funny,' said Oka. 'No, not like a tree.'

At home, Satoya's wife, Sujami, brought them tea and showed photographs of the family in Darwin.

'The youngest son is now the biggest,' Mr Satoya said proudly. 'Because he eat Australian steaks.'

'Darwin is a wonderful place,' said Sujami, pouring them another cup of tea.

The house – very modern by Balinese standards – was replete with towels of Darwin, plaques of Darwin, and a Darwin teapot embossed with a map of Darwin.

'Have you seen the ducks, walking at dusk?' Mr Satoya took them out into the street, and there in the sunset was a triangle of ducks following a duck shepherd who carried a white flag on a stick.

'They are led by a magic pole,' Mr Satoya said. 'They stay by the flag in the rice fields all day until the man comes back.'

'What if someone else tries to steal them?' asked Grafton.

'They won't go if a different man picks up the pole.'

'Smart ducks,' said Grafton. 'What happens if the duck boy dies during the day?'

Mr Satoya was temporarily at a loss for words.

'That does not happen,' he said at last. 'Oh, no,' he said thoughtfully, 'that would not happen.'

Oka and Mr Satoya drove them to see Mr Satoya's resting place. It was being built on a plot of Mr Satoya's family land. The rest of the rice field Mr Satoya rented out to a share farmer. 'He takes 30 per cent, government takes 15 per cent, I take 55 per cent,' said Mr Satoya. It seemed he was something of an entrepreneur.

'I build this house for Australian friends,' he explained. 'They pay for the cost of everything and come here for holidays.'

'But foreigners can't own land,' Janet said.

'Oh, well,' said Mr Satoya, laughing, 'they come here whenever they want, providing they let me know first.'

'Who owns the house when they die?' asked Grafton.

'We have not talked of that,' said Mr Satoya vaguely.

The couple were already sixty-five.

'It seems like a good idea. Where did you think of it?' asked Grafton.

'In Darwin,' answered the teacher. Darwin had taught him a great deal.

'We must go now,' said Mr Satoya, standing on his raised land, the lord of much he surveyed. 'Insects come soon.'

'I'm allergic to midges,' answered Grafton.

'Thank you for speaking English with me.'

'Thank you,' said Janet bowing low. Grafton could tell she did not exactly approve. Still, the rice fields and coconut palms looked very beautiful.

'Someone's moved in next door,' thundered Grafton. 'A whole family by the sound of it. Our holiday will be ruined.'

'Try to let go, my love,' replied Janet, unperturbed. 'Everything will work out, just you wait and see.'

'I knew someone would come,' cried Grafton.

'At least it means the air strike is over,' Janet said brightly. 'Come on, let's have something to eat. The gong went five minutes ago and it could be black rice pudding,' Janet added enticingly.

Grafton sat glumly sucking on his esdjurek while Michael told Janet all about the tragic love of Mimi and Rudolphe.

'A poet and a seamstress. I think *La Boheme* sounds *wonderful*,' enthused Janet.

'What's the point of singing when she's got consumption?' interrupted Grafton.

'Pardon,' said Michael.

'What's the point of Mimi singing when she's so weak and ill? She really shouldn't sing at all.'

Janet and Michael looked nonplussed.

'I read that in a book,' explained Grafton crossly. 'It was meant to be a joke. A joke,' he repeated, reaching for the rice.

A small balding man entered the far end of the restaurant accompanied by an extremely attractive young woman, and a freckled-faced teenage girl.

'That must be the new people,' pointed Grafton.

'How *dare* they move in next to us. There are lots of other rooms in the Tjuamphuan.'

'They can move in next to me any time,' announced Michael, as the girl with her freckled, ready smile bounded eagerly up to him.

'Hi,' said an unaffected Australian voice. 'I'm Jackie.'

'How old are you?' she said, poking Michael playfully in the gut.

'Old enough,' replied Michael with a smile.

'Michael!' reproved Janet.

The girl laughed and put her arms around the director's neck.

'I'm here with my Dad and my step-mum Monica,' she gestured to the table at the end of the room.

'And how old are *you*?' asked Grafton sternly.

'I'm nearly fourteen,' Jackie said.

'Is he your son?' she questioned, putting a wad of chewing gum in her ample mouth and playing with the stubble on Michael's chin.

'Jackie,' came a stern, high-pitched voice from the table at the end of the room. The balding man walked vigorously towards their table.

'Jackie,' shrieked her father, 'come here this *instant.*'

'See you later,' said Jackie, looking directly at Michael. 'I *will* see you later, won't I?' she implored.

Red-faced, Michael shook his head then nodded as the father approached, puffing.

'Name's Jack Turner,' said the bald man. 'From Brisbane,' he said proffering his hand in a very aggressive way.

'Pleased to meet you, I'm sure,' mumbled Michael.

'You've met Jackie, I see,' he said, eyeing his daughter's disappearing form.

'I don't suppose we'll be seeing much of each other,' mused Jack Turner, Brisbane businessman. 'But have a good time anyway,' he said and moved away.

'What a strange man,' said Janet.

'She's got the hots for you,' announced Grafton in disbelief. 'And she's not even fourteen. That was *disgusting,*' he emphasised, wading into some pork.

'She did seem rather keen,' Janet giggled.

'I'd be careful if I were you,' moralised Grafton. 'I've seen her type before,' he said, without a smile. '*And* her father's,' he added menacingly.

'Take my advice and stay right away.' Grafton stood up, looking like a missionary. 'I don't approve at all.'

'Her father's right on to you,' he continued. 'His name's Jack. Hers is Jackie. It suggests to me that her dad thinks he has got a claim on her. It does not augur well, just you mark my words.'

'Come on,' said Michael. 'Let's listen to the cricket summary.' He flicked on his enormous transistor. 'England's won again,' he said with a satisfied smile.

'It seems to be your lucky night,' smiled Janet, apportioning the black rice pudding.

'Depends how you count,' said Grafton severely. 'It depends how you count.'

'Those buggers are really in a trance,' Grafton announced as they watched the Kris dance. 'They're really stabbing themselves.'

'Wait till you see what's next,' said Janet excitedly. 'You see, tourism hasn't hurt the Balinese at all. They get paid for doing what they want to do. What they have to do.'

Out of the temple came an old Balinese priest dressed in white. He had one very long fingernail on his right hand. He anointed a man holding a rocking horse. In the middle of the ground was a huge bonfire of coconut husks which two attendants distributed evenly over the floor.

'This is called the Fire Dance,' said Janet in a hush.

The man, head held back, pranced in and out, kicking the flaming coconuts with his bare feet. Then he stomped on the flames and kicked the burning shells this way and that.

'I hope we don't get hurt,' whispered Grafton, shielding his eyes.

At the end of a crescendo of stomping, the priest snapped the man out of the trance, sprinkling him with holy water. He sat dazed, waiting to be inspected by the tourists.

'I wonder if those shells are really hot?' said Grafton.

'I wouldn't touch them if I were you, my love. You might get burnt,' said Janet.

'Don't be silly,' he snapped in reply, making a desultory kick at an ember. Grafton was wearing thongs.

'I've hurt my foot,' he cried. 'I've burnt my toe.'

'You'll be alright when you feel better, my love.' Janet held his hand.

Oka drove them into Ubud.

'You tell the doctor you are a friend of Mr Satoya,' said Oka. 'He live next door.'

'I hope he knows what he's doing,' said Grafton.

'Of course he does, my love. That's why he is a doctor.'

At the Ubud Clinic, the Balinese doctor, a young, serious man, dressed in white, asked Grafton how he was.

'Not very well, Doctor,' he whimpered. 'It started with my toe, but now I've got this rash on my left thigh and a terrible pain in my side, here,' he grimaced, pointing.

'I see,' said the Doctor, smiling. 'Are there any other symptoms?'

'I've got an ulcer in my mouth,' said Grafton, opening his mouth. 'And a very sore throat. I've got arthritis in the small of my back and in my neck, and I feel nauseous. Every breath is an effort.' Grafton whimpered. 'Is it serious?' 'Oh, well,' said the doctor who had examined him thoroughly. 'I think not, but I will give you an anti-spasm injection for the pain and some antibiotics for the burn and rash.'

'I can't take drugs,' Grafton cried, in anguish. 'I'm allergic to antibiotics.'

His eyes were wide with panic. 'Tell him, Janet.'

Janet explained, and the doctor again smiled.

'These will not hurt you.'

'Must I take them?' implored Grafton.

'It is best,' the doctor said.

'But is it *dangerous*?' Grafton asked.

'I think not,' repeated the doctor emptying the syringe. 'Do not worry. It is distressing, but not dangerous.'

'Take the tablets and do not swim,' announced the doctor, holding out his hand.

'How much do I owe you?' said Grafton. 'I am a friend of Mr Satoya's.'

'1000 Rupiah,' said the doctor.

'That is very reasonable,' said Janet. 'Trima Kasih.'

After paying the fee, they walked slowly into Ubud, arm in arm.

'I feel trapped again,' said Grafton. 'He's told me to take the antibiotics, but we know what happens when I do. I feel terrible,' said Grafton, kicking the ground. 'What do you think I should do?'

'You must learn to let go,' Janet said. 'Oh, look at those statues. Look at those wood carvings. Can we look? Can we?'

'Oh very well,' said Grafton testily. 'But don't you care about me?'

'Of course I do.' Janet lovingly held a Rama and Sita, while Grafton sat crossly outside waiting.

After five minutes, the owner, Noman, approached him. 'It means Number One,' interjected Janet quietly.

'Number One, son,' said Noman proudly. 'This is my brother Made. He Number Two.'

Made held a delicate wooden animal.

'You want to buy Golden Deer? Very cheap – 35,000 Rupiah.' He brought the animal close. Noman could tell that Grafton really liked the deer.

'You like deer?' said Noman smiling. 'For you, special, 33,000.'

'Too dear,' said Grafton, holding his head.

'How much you pay?' said Noman.

'Five thousand Rupiah,' said Grafton, holding his outstretched hand in the air.

'Oh, no,' said Noman, turning away. 'I bought this myself, three years ago for 13,000 Rupiah. I walked fifty miles into the forest.'

'Why didn't you catch a Bemo?' asked Janet.

Grafton and Noman laughed. Made frowned. 'Roads too steep, too rough.'

'All the way through the forest?' cried Grafton, acting out dragging the deer behind him. Made did not smile.

'How much profit you give me?' said Noman.

'Ten thousand Rupiah,' boomed Grafton, holding up both hands. A crowd had gathered to watch.

'Oh, no,' said Made, aggrieved. 'But for you 25,000.'

'Too dear, too dear,' resounded Grafton, putting on

128

his hat. 'Perhaps I come back tomorrow.' The Number One son showed him to the door.

'My leg seems a little better,' said Grafton as they walked jauntily along. 'That injection seems to have done the trick,' Janet said.

'You know, I enjoyed that,' announced Grafton. 'I *want* that Golden Deer.'

'I know, my love. We'll come back tomorrow and bargain some more.'

'It's satay tonight,' said Grafton as they approached the Tjuamphuan. 'I'm hungry. I hope there's black rice pudding for dessert.'

'So do I, my love,' said Janet, putting her head on his shoulder. 'Aren't we having a wonderful holiday?'

'Don't forget to take your malaria tablet,' reminded Grafton, pulling the curtains of their bungalow closed. 'It's Friday.'

'Lekas, Lekas, Satra,' said Grafton, clapping his hands. And hurry indeed Satra did, with tea for three in a huge flowered teapot.

'*Bagoos*,' Grafton emphasised in a very real way.

'Hurry' and 'good' were the extent of Grafton's linguistic accomplishments. Satra smiled. 'You very funny,' said the boy, 'very funny man.'

Michael arrived, clad in a batik shirt with a towel wrapped around his midriff. 'I hope you haven't been seeing that girl again,' Grafton said severely, as he squeezed a lemon into his tea.

'Again,' said Michael, feigning innocence. 'What girl?'

'That girl,' said Grafton with annoyance. 'Seeing her will do you no good at all. I'll tell you that right now. Her father's sure to know . . . If he doesn't know already.' It was beginning to be an obsession with him. 'And if he does, God help you. I think you *have* been seeing her,' Grafton persisted as Michael looked away.

Liger, Michael's fifty year-old boy, brought his freshly ironed sarong.

129

'You can't wear that,' said Grafton. 'You'll look like a gypsy.'

'We're going to the Bali Hyatt,' emphasised Grafton, 'not to Ubud village.'

'For a free meal,' laughed Janet, who emerged out of the bungalow wearing a traditional blue woven sarong and a yellow hibiscus in her hair.

'You look lovely,' said Grafton, pointing to her tea. 'I still feel guilty about winning,' he frowned.

'It wasn't your fault,' said Janet, stroking his hand.

'I'll be paying for mine,' said Michael, trying to help. 'We'll have a grand time.'

'As long as you don't wear that sarong,' said Grafton.

'Let Michael wear what he wants,' retorted Janet.

'We don't have much time,' said Grafton, glancing at his wrist. They all laughed as Grafton realised he hadn't worn a watch for days.

As they walked to the car, Jackie hid behind the Banyan tree. Wearing a loud batik shirt and tight matching shorts, she mischievously waved Michael goodbye. The Englishman pretended not to notice.

'I saw that,' said Grafton. 'No doubt her Dad did too. It's a disgrace.'

On the way into Denpassar, Grafton, sitting in the front beside Oka, turned around. 'Best make sure of our reservations. You know what Garuda are like.'

'Fine by me,' replied Michael nonchalantly.

'*My big fear*,' Grafton emphasised to Janet, 'is that we'll be stuck here and we won't be able to get out.'

'There could be worse fates,' laughed Michael.

'You don't have to get to Sydney until New Year. But I've got to be back in Brisbane by Christmas. It's my birthday.'

'Look at the paddyfields,' said Janet, with delight, 'and look at that temple.'

'I have to know,' growled Grafton.

'Oh, well,' said Janet gently. It was her way of soothing him. 'If it makes you feel better.'

At the Garuda office, Grafton wasn't making much progress.

'I need an answer,' he screamed. 'I need to know if the flight is *definitely* going. I can't bear uncertainty,' he explained to the Garuda official, who, shaking his head from side to side, smiled.

'Let's go and get our free meal,' said Janet. 'You always feel better with a full stomach.'

'But when will I *know*,' he lamented.

'Difficult to say,' said Michael, in a lordly way.

'It's Bali time,' said Janet.

'Oh, yes, Bali time,' reinforced Oka, eyes lighting up. His large white teeth shone.

'Don't worry, my love, everything will work out fine.'

'Hello, I'm Doctor Everest,' announced Grafton. 'My wife and I have won the Funtastic Free Meal and Cultural Night. I'd like to book a table for three – my young friend will pay for himself.'

'The evening meal does not begin until seven,' said the dining room attendant, without looking up. He was Eurasian.

'But that's over an hour,' boomed Grafton. 'I'm hungry.'

'Then may I suggest that sir goes to the coffee lounge or has a drink in the bar.'

'I don't drink alcohol,' informed Grafton.

'I do,' said Michael.

'Let's book our table and get a snack,' said Janet brightly.

'They didn't seem at all pleased to see us,' said Grafton, crossly.

'Perhaps not all the winners collect,' laughed Michael, leading him away.

'I'm thirsty,' said Grafton, as they sat at a poolside table. 'I'd like a mango and avocado juice – like we had last week in Denpassar.' Grafton licked his lips.

A small Balinese waiter, dressed in a brown uniform, approached smiling. He handed Janet the menu.

131

'What sort of *pure* fruit juice do you have?' questioned Grafton.

'Oh, yes, fruit juice,' smiled the waiter.

'What *sort* of fruit juice?' asked Grafton, raising his voice. 'What flavours?'

The waiter smiled uncomprehendingly and walked away.

'This is ridiculous,' screamed Grafton. 'Tell him I want a mango and avocado juice.'

'I think,' said Michael looking at the menu, 'that they only have one fruit juice – it's probably a mixture.'

'That's ridiculous,' said Grafton. 'This is the Bali Hyatt.'

'Find out,' said Grafton, menacingly, to Janet who was caught midway between the waiter and their table.

Janet came back rather sheepishly. 'He said,' said Janet, stifling a giggle, 'that they have fruit juice, so I've ordered three.'

'How *dare* you,' screamed Grafton, thumping the table. 'How dare you not get what I want. I'm leaving,' said Grafton, storming to his feet. 'I'm going back to the Tjuamphuan.'

'But you can't,' said Janet sweetly. 'You've given Oka the night off and told him to come back at ten-thirty.'

'Oh, Christ,' said Grafton, wrenching off his hat.

'So that we can have a night out and enjoy ourselves. Why don't you just sit down,' persisted Janet, 'and calm yourself?'

'Here come the drinks,' said Michael brightly. 'Let me get them. How much?'

'Yes, fruit juice,' said the waiter. 'Fruit juice,' he said, placing the long yellow-orange liquid before them.

'This is delicious,' said Janet. 'Delicious. It's got everything in it – banana, papaya . . . and mango,' she said remembering.

'It's not bad,' said Grafton testily, tasting his drink. 'Not bad at all,' he said, eyes brightening. 'In fact, I think it's *mainly* mango and avocado. After this,' he

132

said, draining his glass, 'we'll go for a walk along the beach. It's good for the appetite. After all, we are on holidays.'

As they entered the huge open-air restaurant at 7 p.m. precisely, a raised stage garlanded with flowers faced them. To the right were tiers and tiers of food decorated with palm fronds and more flowers. Many, many servants stood beside the tables which stretched for twenty metres. A chef was stationed next to each silver cauldron containing hot food – roasted meat, sweet and sour fish, prawns and shrimp and lobster, while at the end of the line was a pile of brightly-coloured coconut cakes – lime-green and pink. Apart from the staff, they were the only people there. 'It must be a smorgasbord,' said Janet, in awe. 'I wish I hadn't eaten lunch.'

'I'm going to have some roast pig,' said Grafton, smacking his lips. 'I'm glad we're here first.'

'I think there'll be enough for everyone,' laughed Michael, surveying the mountain of food.

'One can keep going back for more,' said Grafton, stuffing in his roast pig. 'It's an excellent idea, having an Indonesian night.'

Grafton acknowledged two plump American ladies and a large single man who had separately waddled in.

'I'm glad there's not many here,' he said, sumptuously. 'I hate a crowd.'

The gamelan orchestra, the largest they had seen, started to play.

'The Cultural Night is about to begin,' said Michael, consulting his programme. 'I might get some ideas.'

'You don't need ideas,' interjected Grafton. 'What you need,' pointing his fork at the Englishman's nose, 'is discipline and restraint.'

'It's the Ramayana,' explained Janet. 'It's supposed to be very good.'

Two exquisite Balinese, dressed in embroidered gold brocade and crowned with flowers, began a long and supple dance.

133

'Look at their hands,' exclaimed Janet. 'See how they hold their fingers.'

'In a trance,' said Janet, 'very young girls with no training at all can perform the Legong in unison. Isn't that amazing?'

'It's not as amazing as that fire dance,' remarked Grafton, his mouth very full. After some uncertainty all three laughed. As Rama and Sita and the other characters appeared, Janet explained that the story was a symbolic struggle of good and evil. Grafton and Michael munched appreciatively. Throughout the dance they went back for more.

'He's hardly eaten a thing,' said Grafton, pointing to the unattached man.

'Perhaps he comes in every night,' Michael said.

'Even so it seems a shame.'

'There's Haññumañ, the good white monkey,' exclaimed Janet, as the men sat down. 'Isn't he lovely?'

'It certainly is impressive,' replied Michael. 'Look at his tail.'

'There's a *Golden Deer*,' said Grafton, leaping to his feet. Still pointing, he leant down to pick up his napkin. 'I really *want* that Golden Deer,' he said seriously.

'Well, we'll go back tomorrow, my love.'

'I think it's got *shot*,' cried Grafton.

'It's all part of the story,' said Janet. 'Actually, it's a good sign. It means Sita will soon be rescued.'

As the Ramayana drew to a close, Grafton got another plate of multi-coloured cakes and some mint chocolates to have with their coffee. He had just sat down when the ketjak dance began, with over a hundred chanting men playing the part of monkeys.

'I think Rangda the witch queen has stirred them up,' said Michael, trying to read the programme.

'It looks like a gigantic sea anemone,' said Janet.

'Indeed it does,' assented Grafton, reaching for another cake. 'These are good,' he said, passing a green one to his friend.

'Isn't this lovely,' exclaimed Janet.

134

'Indeed it is,' said Grafton. 'I really feel quite content.'

'To Bali,' said Michael, proposing a toast.

'To Bali.' They drank their coffee and happily left.

'I feel sick,' complained Grafton, as Oka thundered them home. 'I've eaten too much,' he persisted.

'Don't grizzle,' said Michael from the back seat. 'We've had a wonderful time.'

'Look at the villages as we pass,' said Janet. 'Almost everyone's asleep.'

'I wish I was back in Brisbane,' lamented Grafton. 'I miss my pussy. I wonder what she's doing now?'

'I hope they've kept my black rice pudding,' he said as they neared the Tjuamphuan. 'I'd like just a little before we go to sleep.'

'I hope not everyone's asleep,' said Michael, leaping out of the car and heading towards his bungalow. 'Thanks for a terrific night,' he called back over his shoulder. 'It's only just begun.'

'What does he mean by that?' Grafton asked. Janet explained.

'Why didn't you keep my black rice pudding?' Grafton asked Satra when breakfast came.

'I waited until ten-thirty and then I went home to my village,' he said. 'I am very sorry. Very sorry. Breakfast is good?' he said hopefully.

'Don't you worry,' Janet said. 'He gets very cross in the mornings,' pointing at Grafton. 'Don't you, my love?'

Grafton grunted.

'Today is the wedding of Liger's brother,' said Satra happily. 'Everyone is invited. You will come?' he said to Janet. 'Yes?'

'Can we go? Oh, can we?' Janet clapped her hands.

'How do we get there?' Grafton asked crossly, eating his omelette.

'In the bemo,' said Satra. 'Tjuamphuan brings two bemos.'

'I get sick in buses.'

'Why don't you ride with me?' boomed Michael, who had just wandered down from his bungalow. 'On my motor bike.' He looked enormously pleased with himself. 'That wasn't very funny last night,' said Grafton. 'I hope you were only joking,' Grafton continued. 'The girl's fourteen,' he said, with shock. Michael helped himself to tea as Satra produced another cup.

'It could be fun,' said Janet, ignoring her husband's interrogation. 'Oh please can we go?'

'How much does it cost?' Grafton asked Satra.

'How much does *what* cost?' laughed Michael.

'The wedding. How much does the wedding cost?'

'Oh, no,' said Satra. 'Wedding cost nothing. You are all invited . . . as guest,' he said. 'Liger would be sad if you did not come.'

'So that settles that,' said Michael, in a very English way.

'Can I bring a present?' said Janet.

'We give present from us all,' Satra explained quietly. 'It is better.

'Well, if we are going, I'd better change,' said Grafton.

He emerged wearing a freshly laundered white cotton shirt, his big floppy hat and a new pair of shorts.

Farewelling Janet, who sat happily in the back of the bemo, Grafton gingerly climbed aboard the bike. He clasped both hands tightly around Michael's stomach, pressing the machine tightly with his knees.

As they passed the King's Palace, Jackie and Monica came into view. Seeing Michael, Jackie licked her lips and waved behind her stepmother's back as Michael accelerated.

'That was disgusting,' called Grafton, from the back of the machine, which was gathering speed.

Silent, Michael looked straight ahead. Temples and statues, shrines and paddyfields whizzed by, walled village enclosures came into sight and went, the inhabitants going slowly about their business in the mid-morning sun.

When they approached a line of school children, Grafton took off his floppy hat and, arms out-stretched, boomed out 'Hello, hello,' as he waved.

'Hello, hello,' came the echoed reply. Hordes of children appeared. On the back of Michael's Yamaha, Grafton noisily clapped his hands. The hordes of running children did likewise.

'Hello, hello,' boomed Grafton still clapping.

'Hello, hello,' responded the children as the motor cycle went past.

'That was fun. I'm really enjoying myself,' Grafton cried out, craning forward.

'Good on you,' responded Michael, gathering speed. 'So am I.'

By the time they found the wedding it was noon. The bemo had already arrived. As they entered the compound, Grafton beheld a mosaic of flowers and brightly-dyed rice. A carpet of offerings lay on the ground, and from the beams above hung palm leaf streamers. Among the Balinese guests moved tourists with cameras. Directly in front of the bride stood Janet, eyes wide with excitement.

'Isn't she having a good time,' said Grafton, proudly. 'She really is very beautiful.'

As the ceremony began, Grafton focused on the bride. Wearing a fine orange top and a batik sarong, she held a dish, with flowers in a banana leaf, while an old woman – presumably her mother – dressed her hair in a bun. The wedding priest and a monk hovered in the background, sprinkling water. There was no music or chanting. The bride managed a cross smile for the photographing tourists, all the while ignoring the thin groom who seemed very young and tentative. Liger and Oka and Oka II and most of the Tjuamphuan staff smiled approvingly in the background, drinking rice wine, as the ceremony slowly – very slowly – unfolded.

'She doesn't seem terribly happy,' Michael whispered in Grafton's ear.

'She's a reluctant bride all right,' Grafton announced

to anyone who would care to hear. 'It's probably a shot-gun. I need to find a toilet,' he added loudly in a surly voice. 'I think I've got the runs.' A host showed him the way.

After nearly overbalancing on his haunches, Grafton crossly emerged from the toilet. The wedding appeared not to have advanced at all.

'It takes a day,' Janet explained as he passed.

Grafton resumed his position with Michael and asked his host for more soft drink and a chair. Suddenly, Grafton felt hot and unhappy and enclosed. 'We're going to have to leave,' he announced. 'I feel sick.' 'But I'm enjoying myself,' replied the Englishman, who had demolished four glasses of wine.

'I feel sick,' repeated Grafton. 'I have to go.'

Grafton clung unsteadily on the motor bike, hat pulled down over his head, fat legs exposed to the sun as they taxied into the Tjuamphuan.

'I've got a sore throat and terrible sunburn,' croaked Grafton, as he vomited into the hole in the bungalow's bathroom.

'Look at my legs.'

'Oh, well,' said Satra, who had remained behind, 'I will bring up an esdjeruk.'

When Grafton awoke at dusk, Janet was hovering above him.

'The wedding was wonderful,' she said. 'Almost as wonderful as ours, but so different.'

'I feel sick. I've got a sore throat and . . .'

'I know, my love. Here, gargle with this.' Janet produced some Disprin in a glass and a handful of Vitamin C.

'I hope I don't get a strep throat,' he whined.

'Try not to panic, my love.'

'I've got to go to the toilet,' cried Grafton, getting to his feet. 'I've been four times since this morning.'

'When you're finished,' called Janet, 'take two Lomotil. They'll fix you up. Fast tonight. You'll be right as rain in the morning.'

'*Fast*,' whimpered a voice from the bathroom below. 'What about my black rice pudding?'

'That papaya was delicious,' said Grafton. 'Although my throat is still sore, I'm feeling much better this morning.' Grafton had on his floppy hat, white shirt and long pants. Noman was waiting for them. The deer was outside the shop.

'For you,' called Noman, 'twenty-two thousand.'

'Nine thousand,' said Grafton, fingers raised.

'Oh, no,' said Noman, with a puzzled smile. 'Last time you say ten thousand'

'Very well, ten thousand,' said Grafton sternly, hands behind his back.

'Twenty thousand cheap price,' said Noman, turning away.

As the bargaining continued, Made, sitting on his haunches, and Made's wife, resting on a motor bike, looked on intently.

'You give me no profit,' said Noman, bringing out a garish Garuda bird. 'For you, eight thousand.'

'That's terrible,' said Grafton in disgust. 'Take it away.'

'You want Rama?' questioned Made, bringing out a large figure. 'For you, ten thousand.'

'It's nice,' said Grafton, turning Prince Rama upside down. 'But I want the Golden Deer.'

'Eleven thousand five hundred,' said Grafton, taking off his hat.

'Eighteen thousand,' said Noman.

'Twelve thousand,' said Grafton, looking at Janet.

'Seventeen thousand,' said Noman.

'Twelve thousand five hundred is my final price,' said Grafton, taking Janet by the arm.

'Oh, no,' intoned Noman. 'For twelve thousand five hundred you can have Prince Rama and Garuda bird. Cheap price.'

'I want the Golden Deer,' said Grafton, tears in his eyes. 'For twelve thousand five hundred.'

'Very sorry,' said Noman, taking the deer inside.

'We're going,' threatened Grafton, reluctantly walking away. He took five paces, then turned around. 'Thirteen thousand,' he said. 'That is my final price'.

'For you,' said Noman, 'fourteen thousand.'

'Thirteen thousand five hundred,' said Grafton opening up his wallet.

'Fourteen thousand,' repeated Noman, grinning like a cheshire cat.

'Very well,' said Grafton. 'Fourteen thousand.'

Noman shook his hands. Made and Made's wife and Janet and the children clapped.

'It is very beautiful,' said Grafton, stroking the animal.

'Oh, very beautiful,' said Noman, dismantling the Golden Deer. 'See how ears and horns, legs come off.' Made's wife brought some brown paper and Noman wrapped the purchase very carefully.

'I hope we get it through Customs,' said Grafton.

'Terima Kasih,' she said, as Noman brought the parcel.

'Let's take a picture,' said Grafton, 'of Noman and me and the Golden Deer. And Made and the children too.' Noman smiled and reassembled the animal which he again placed outside.

'Tomorrow, I take you to see my house?'

'If we have time,' said Grafton.

'We will send you a picture,' said Janet. 'From Australia. And one for Made too. Terima Kasih.'

'Bagus,' said Grafton, as they left with the wrapped animal clutched protectively under his arm.

'I'm so pleased I got that Golden Deer,' said Grafton, as they strolled back across the wooden bridge.

'So am I, my love,' said Janet. 'So am I.'

'I feel so tired, I don't really want to go,' said Grafton, sitting on their bed while Janet packed.

'The bungalow's like our home,' she said.

'I'll miss Satra and seeing the tree snake,' said Grafton. 'And Michael. I think I've made a friend.'

'It's nearly time,' said Janet, 'Don't forget ...' she said as Satra walked in, bringing their last bowl of hot water.

'This is for you, Satra,' said Grafton, handing him two 5,000 Rupiah notes. 'You have been very good.'

'Oh, thank you,' said Satra, as Grafton formally shook hands. 'I'd like an esdjeruk before I go. Let's take some pictures,' he said as Janet closed their cases.

Grafton was astonished to find Michael and young Jackie together, waiting for them at the entrance to the Tjuamphuan. Grafton looked crossly at Michael. Using Janet's Instamatic, they took turns taking pictures of Grafton and Janet and Michael and Jackie in front of the huge Banyan tree, which had an altar in its trunk. Michael was wearing beads.

'Oh, smell the frangipanis,' said Janet. 'Look!' A line of Balinese women with decorated offerings tiered on their heads went past the road down to the river.

'It must be a ceremony,' Janet explained.

Janet took a picture of Michael and Jackie with Grafton in the middle, disapproving. Clutching the large brown wallet in which he kept the passports, money and tickets, Grafton looked like a Jehovah's Witness.

As Michael snapped the final picture of Janet and Grafton, Noman arrived, holding the Rama.

'For you,' he said. 'My friends. Very cheap, 10,000 Rupiah. Only for you,' he said.

'We can't fit any more in,' said Janet, who had bought six Village Ming plates from Klungkung.

'Next time,' said Grafton. 'We shall be back.'

'You promise,' said Noman, aggrieved.

'I promise,' said Grafton. 'We have had a wonderful time.'

As Oka arrived with Mr Satoya's taxi, Satra appeared from the bungalow with a red hibiscus, which he gave to Janet. There were tears in his eyes. As they got into the car, Michael kissed Janet goodbye and put his arms around Grafton.

'It's been grand to meet you,' said Michael.

'I'll miss you,' responded Grafton. 'You will come and see us in Brisbane?'

'Of course I will.'

'And take us to *La Boheme*,' said Janet.

'I promise.'

'Here's thirty-five thousand Rupiah,' said Grafton. 'You give us the money in Australian currency.'

Oka switched on the ignition and circled the car around. Satra called out, 'Janet, Grafton, I am really crying.' And so indeed he was.

'Wasn't that lovely?' exclaimed Janet.

'Michael's got his arm around that girl,' Grafton cried in alarm.

'Leave the boy alone,' said Janet, holding his hand. 'He's probably lonely.'

'I don't feel very well,' said Grafton, as they approached the airport.

'You're just excited, my love.'

'Mr Satoya said to say goodbye,' said Oka, smiling brightly as he carried their bags up to the departure lounge.

'You come next year?' said Oka, as Grafton handed him a two thousand Rupiah note.

'We hope so,' said Janet.

'Why is the airport so crowded?' interrogated Grafton, becoming disturbed.

'Probably some planes are late,' said Janet.

'Look,' said Grafton, pointing at the Departure Board. His hand quivered with rage. 'A Qantas and a Garuda Flight are going at the same time. How dare they not tell us,' said Grafton, advancing on the reservation clerk.

'A Qantas flight is going direct to Brisbane, and Garuda goes via Melbourne to Sydney. It's a waste of time,' Grafton said to the confounded clerk. 'And then we'll probably miss our connecting flight.'

'My name is Doctor Everest,' he boomed, holding his Garuda tickets in the air, 'and I want to be transferred

to Qantas. The travel agent didn't tell us we could go
direct to Brisbane. I'm an Australian,' he bellowed.

'Calm down, my love,' said Janet, who explained in
pidgin Bahasa Indonesia what was going on.

'Don't apologise for me,' screamed Grafton. 'I want
to go back on Qantas. I feel sick,' he said to the clerk. 'I
have to go home.'

The Balinese clerk ignored Grafton and smiling at
Janet, said, 'It is possible. I will ring.' Grafton and Janet
waited for ten minutes. He sat, fretting on their suitcases, until his name was called.

'It is done,' said the Balinese with a smile. 'We hope
you come again to Bali.' Grafton carried their bags to
the Qantas counter and weighed them in.

'Very sorry,' said a Balinese voice across the loud-
speaker system. 'Garuda flight 874 delayed two hours
forty-five minutes from Djarkata. Expected time of
departure to Melbourne 12.45 a.m.'

'There, I told you,' said Grafton proudly. 'I knew we'd
done the right thing.'

'Qantas flight 409 now departing.' As they walked on
to the tarmac the same voice said. 'Very sorry, Garuda
flight 874 to Melbourne – Sydney now cancelled.'
Grafton ascended the 747 with a satisfied smile.

'Thank Christ, it's steak,' said Grafton, as the menu
was handed out. 'I'm feeling a bit off colour,' he
explained to the chubby Qantas steward. 'And my legs
are very sore.'

'Don't worry, my love. A good meal will fix you up.'

'How did you know that girl?' asked Janet, clutching
her Dutch-Indonesian lamp.

'I told you,' Grafton answered crossly. 'She was a
student, and not very bright.'

'Are you glad you're married to me?' asked Janet,
snuggling up to him.

'Of course I'm glad, there's no one else I could be
married to.

'I have to go to the toilet,' he said, 'my legs are really
hurting.'

143

In the toilet Grafton saw his thighs and turned white. Checking his bowel movement for blood he stumbled back to their seat.

'I've got terrible sunburn,' he cried excitedly.

'You'll be alright, my love,' Janet nodded absently and continued to read.

'My legs are covered in blisters. Look,' he said, rolling up his pants.

Janet blanched. The blisters on both legs were huge. On the thighs they were as big as tomatoes.

'What can I do?' lamented Grafton.

'You'll just have to hang on,' said Janet, holding his hand. 'It must be the pressure of the air conditioning. How could you have got such terrible sunburn?'

'On the back of Michael's bike,' whined Grafton. 'When I was in shorts.'

'You *will* be alright, my love. We'll just have to hang on until we get to Brisbane.'

'That trip was a nightmare,' said Grafton, as he limped into Customs. 'Every step is agony,' he whimpered.

'*Please* let me go through first,' demanded Grafton. 'I have to see a doctor.'

The customs clerk brought him a collapsible wheelchair and whisked them through. 'Thank God, my deer is safe,' said Grafton wheeling himself away. 'You get the bags, I'll hail a taxi.'

'I hope Dr Head is open,' said Grafton. 'It's Saturday morning and tomorrow's Christmas Eve.'

'Go as fast as you can,' Grafton commanded the driver, a smoker, who, much to Grafton's chagrin, related how he got first degree burns from sunbaking in Cairns, and how they became infected and he had to be hospitalised.

'I'd rather not talk about it,' said Grafton. 'I'm in terrible pain. Just get me there as soon as you can. And put out that cigarette, I feel sick.'

'There's no chance, mate, it's after twelve,' comforted the driver.

144

'Oh, Christ, the surgery's closed,' cried Grafton. 'What am I going to do?'

'Search me,' said the driver.

'Have a good holiday, Doc?' called Mr Oldfield, from the pharmacy.

'Can I see you?' wailed Grafton, clambering out of the taxi. 'I've got terrible burns.'

'My God, you've given yourself a lashing,' said the chemist as Grafton sat in the back in his underpants. 'It looks like someone's poured boiling water over you.'

'Is it serious?' whimpered Grafton.

'Well, it's not good,' laughed Mr Oldfield, examining his thighs. 'But it's not critical, put it that way.' He scratched his bald head and thought. 'Show us your hands.' Grafton lifted up his fat hands for inspection. 'See,' said Mr Oldfield. 'You've lost pigmentation.'

'What's that mean?' said Grafton.

'It means that you're photosensitive, allergic to the sun and light. From the chloroquine, from the malaria tablets.'

'Will it get better?' whined Grafton. 'What can I do?'

'Well,' he said to Janet, who had paid the taxi driver and brought all their cases in, 'bathe him every two hours with iced water and Condy's Crystals, and make sure he stays inside out of the sun and light for two weeks. Because,' he said to Grafton, 'if you get more sun on that it could be irreversible.'

'Irreversible?' said Grafton.

'The loss of pigmentation,' said Mr Oldfield. 'I know a bloke in Brisbane,' he continued, 'who has to wear a face mask and white goggles because he didn't do as he was told.'

'But tomorrow's Christmas Day,' whined Grafton. 'It's my birthday.'

'Well, you'll just have to celebrate in bed,' said the chemist. 'That shouldn't be too difficult.'

Grafton and Che lay in bed. Blisters as big as tomatoes had come up on his knees and hands as well.

'I'm held together by a wish,' he said to Che, who

lay on her back purring, as Janet brought his tray.

'Don't worry, you're safe at home,' said Janet, giving him a kiss. 'Happy Birthday.' He blew out the candle on the richly-decorated chocolate cake and looked at the Golden Deer which stood at the foot of the bed in front of the colour television.

'That was a good holiday,' he said to Janet. 'I even enjoyed it while I was there.'

'I knew you would,' she said, putting aside the tray.

'It's a shame about these burns,' he said as he tickled Che underneath her chin.

'Everything happens for a reason,' said Janet.

'Perhaps I could get the invalid pension,' Grafton mused.

'Of course you could, my love. Why don't you have a little something to eat? It'll make you feel better.'

Do You Remember, Miss Plover?

Grafton liked Albert Brunston. They were both outsiders. His dad Bill Everest was a lapsed Catholic, while his English mother Avis had doubts.

Albert Brunston was a Jew. He had the biggest head Grafton had ever seen. His Dad and Mum were both doctors who had come to Australia as refugees. Mister's medical qualifications were accepted immediately but Mrs Brunston had to pass the exams. Albert and Grafton were at little school and big school together. In third grade – Miss Plover's class – Albert was known as a brain.

He and Grafton were both only children having had elder brothers who'd died when young. While Avis said Grafton was 'quite pretty' before he started having asthma, Albert's Mum, Dr Brunston, told almost everyone she met how *ugly* Albert had been as a baby. She had even been ashamed of being seen wheeling her big-headed son in the pram. As a consequence, while Grafton often stayed home sick, Albert retreated into 'being smart'. Avis insisted her son was named Grafton after the town, not the gaol: his Dad said he'd worked there as a boy before he came to Melbourne to play football.

Every morning Albert, who had memorised a page of the *Children's Encyclopedia* the night before, used to intimidate Miss Plover. 'What is the speed of light?' said Albert, putting up his hand. Miss Plover wouldn't know. 'The speed of light is 860,000 miles per hour,' said Albert, smiling brilliantly. 'How long does it take light to get to the sun? Six minutes, Miss,' Albert answered without pause, as their teacher shook her head. 'How many hairs on a person's head?' 'I don't know,' Miss Plover mourned. 'x hairs for blond, y hairs for a red head,' said Albert proudly. Each morning Albert would pour out his questions and answer them himself.

One day Miss Plover got her own back when Albert was out of the room. She confided to the class: 'Don't tell Albert Brunston, but when he's eighteen, his brain is going to burst.'

Of course, the children relayed this news with alacrity. To understate the case, it made a huge impact on Albert.

Two days later Albert found out that his real name was Brunstein. For the sake of the practice, Doctor Mr had changed his name to Brunston. The news had a devastating effect on Albert. All the other kids jeered, calling him 'Broomstick, Broomstick.' Only Bill Powers from across the street and Grafton told him it didn't matter. 'Brunstein. It's just a *name*.' Bill's now a psychiatrist – at Beechworth. He is an Orange Person.

After third grade Albert was never the same again. He slowed down. Never lived up to his promise. That was because he was afraid to try. He was terrified of thinking, of using, exercising, actually *exerting* his brain, unless the effort made it burst.

Now, twice married, an unemployed anthropologist, Albert is worried about his loss of memory. He blames too much alcohol. Albert is cutting down on fat. He even tried the Pritikin diet. But *we* know where the fault lies, don't we? We blame, quite rightly, *Miss Plover*.

Wherever you are, if your nieces or nephews are readers, Miss Plover, *I hope you are ashamed*.

You should go to Albert's house in East Brighton, Melbourne, and look into his haunted face. His brain is bursting inside, ever so slowly, bleeding away, running down, one day at a time, as a punishment for making you feel like a fool.

Miss Plover, dribbling away in some old people's

home, aren't you *ashamed*? And what about Grafton?
Do you remember, when he played Big Billygoat Gruff?
He tried too hard and hurt Bessie Bigboots who played
the Troll, by butting her very hard . . . in that place. He
didn't mean to hurt her. To make her cry. And even if he
did? So what? But you called him a 'Bully' in front of
everyone. And when Grafton asked about multiplication
by nought, you made him feel ashamed. We'll come back
to that. How *do* you multiply three apples by no apples?

In third form at Forest Hill High Albert was getting very
disturbed. At the Parents' Night, Mr Sorrell, their form
teacher (he had actually been a communist, in Tasmania)
was so worried about Albert that he asked to see his
parents. Only Doctor Mrs Brunston came. Doctor Mister
Brunston had to mind the practice in St Kilda.

Mister Sorrell told Grafton this last year. He teaches
now at La Trobe.

'I was worried about Albert,' he explained. 'I said
to his mother "I'm quite concerned about Albert's
behaviour".'

Mrs Brunston replied, 'But is he a good boy?'

Mr Sorrell persisted, 'I really am quite concerned
about young Albert.'

To which Doctor Mrs Brunston said, 'But does he do
as he's told? Is he a good boy?'

'What could I say?' Mr Sorrell said. There was really
no response.

This year Albert is restarting his PhD at Monash. But he
has such difficulty remembering, I don't think he'll get it
done. Doctor Mr Brunston died years ago. But Doctor
Mrs Brunston, she remarried a gentile, is now seventy
five and still in practice three days a week at St Kilda.
She owns two houses and four flats. Albert and his
childless, pale American Protestant wife came to
Melbourne from Sydney four years ago. He resigned
from a job at the University of New South Wales. The
day after they made him a Senior Lecturer. Albert and

his second wife have just paid off the mortgage on their house in East Brighton by a gift from Mrs Brunston. Some Gift!

At first, to save tax Mrs Brunston put one of the flats in Albert's name. Albert had to collect the $100 a week rent and take it over to his Mum once a fortnight.

After Albert resigned from the University of New South Wales he took a job as a Research Officer with the Liberal Party in Melbourne. But six months after, they lost the State Election. And Albert lost his job. Anyway, Albert is too much of a maverick to keep to the Party (any party) line. He even wanted to produce a *Liberal Star*. Like Pete Steedman's Labour magazine. Steedman and Grafton were at Monash together. We saw him on TV again last night. He came across remarkably well.

Whatever they might say about Albert, even though he's afraid of thinking, he's got an independent mind. And he's loyal. He still talks about School. Big school and little school and especially Forest Hill High.

Last year Albert was short of money. So he presented Doctor Mrs Brunston with a package she couldn't refuse.

Albert explained that, what with tax, his mother *actually* got very little for rent.

But if he (Albert) sold the flat, paid off his mortgage, bought him and his pale American wife a new car, bought a computer, had a few household repairs done to their East Brighton home, *and paid Doctor Mrs Brunston $100 a week cash in hand*, his mother would be *$50-a-week better off, for ever*.

All Albert and his wife have to do is find $200 each fortnight and take it to kind, good, generous Mrs Brunston. As it happens, that's not so easy.

'And if you don't come up with the money?' Grafton wheezed, wide-eyed and eager over dinner (an excellent meal) at Albert's place last week.

He was, it must be admitted, rather subdued as Grafton had just claimed to have fingered the cause of

his memory problems as none other than Miss Plover.
(Where, I wonder, is that huge shrieking girl who played
the Troll to Grafton's Big Billygoat Gruff. Did she ever
have children? Did she marry even? Did he ruin her
future? Turn her into a dyke?) 'I don't think she'd *really*
mind,' said Albert talking about his mother. 'Oh, no,'
said his wife. 'I hate it. Hate being indebted to her
gratitude.'

'One gets nothing for nothing,' Grafton explained
unhelpfully and accepted some more roast beef.

'Have you seen your mother?' asked Albert trying to
change the subject. Albert knew, but his wife didn't,
that Grafton seldom sees his Mum. 'Avis doesn't know
I'm down,' he explained. 'This meat is delicious.' 'Why
not?' asked Albert's childless wife from the half-
renovated kitchen. 'I hate her,' said Grafton. 'Loathe
her. Wish she were dead.'

'That's awful,' said Albert. 'My mother would throw
you out of the house.' Albert had actually written a poem
entitled 'Mother' in third grade. Some classmate found it
and laughed. He never wrote another. 1954 wasn't a
good year.

'I wrote a poem about Avis,' Grafton said. 'It got
published last year.'

'I'm pleased,' said Albert.

'Could we hear it?' asked Albert's wife.

'I don't think it'd be your cup of tea,' he said cheer-
fully. 'But here goes:

> Your sign is shrapnel:
> 'No Entry' splintered in a cold white light.
> I sodomize all trespassers,
> Huddle like a sentry in the dark.
> Your death will not set the seal,
> O blind and two-faced,
> withered and mutilating angel
> I forgive you
> mother can you hear me?
> What colour are your eyes?

'That's terrible,' said Albert after a long silence. 'It's so *cruel*.'

Albert then explained that his first wife's father – a horrible man – had been a Nazi sympathizer during the war.

But Doctor Mrs Brunston insisted that Albert be nice to his father-in-law. *Love for Parents (any parents)* was a *sacred rule*. (As sacred as, in fact more sacred than, the rule that professors – all professors – are worthy of respect.) So love for Parent (any parent) overcame Doctor Mrs Brunston's Jewish pride.

After Grafton had a large second helping of apple pie, Albert drove him to the airport. He had to fly home to Brisbane.

During the drive Albert told Grafton about Barry Anders – another boy in their final year at Forest Hill High. Barry was incurably ill in a mental hospital. 'At least *we're* hanging in there,' Grafton said with a laugh.

'Next year we're having a Twenty-Fifth Anniversary Dinner of the Cohort of 1963 – our sixth form, all 250 of us,' enthused Albert. 'Barry Anders won't be able to come.' Shaking hands, they decided to buy a lottery ticket. Called it 'School'.

'Do you remember? . . .,' asked Albert as Grafton struggled out of the car.

Another's Trouble

'He was tall and slim, with stooping shoulders, induced, no doubt, by a habit of leaning forward to assist his very defective eyesight. His walk was very awkward ... his features were small, while the contour of his face reminded me of Byron's ... When alone he used to saunter along slowly, very seldom putting his horse out of walk. I believe now that it was at these times he was composing his poetry. He hinted this to me, but I never could get him to show me any of his compositions.'

A hard white light settled on the cemetery as Grafton unpicked the gate in Hawthorn Road. He ushered Marie through. She was to get married tomorrow.

Marie had brought him a brown woollen jumper she had knitted as a farewell. A dreamy lad, Grafton wore that jumper for ages.

He took her to Adam Lindsay Gordon's grave. They held hands in front of Gordon's plain tomb, backed by an evergreen hedge, and looked at the broken column, bearing a marble laurel wreath, which the poet's admirers had erected: 'Life is only froth and bubble, two things stand like stone, kindness in another's trouble, courage in your own.'

Marie loved him in a way, but had assessed the situation realistically – Grafton Everest, at least at this stage, was not marriage material.

Marie's father was a minister – the Reverend Barry Victa. So was the man she was to marry, Gordon Holmes, a tutor at the University. After the wedding they would go to Oxford where Gordon, a self-opinionated prig Grafton thought, was to do postgraduate studies in divinity. The Reverend Victa liked Grafton a lot. A bit of an oddball, Barry ran the Presbyterian Church at Monbulk. There were never more than ten parishioners. He took Grafton three times to hear a faith-healer – Brother Mandus – when he came to Melbourne. Brother Mandus's magazine of faith followed Grafton around the world – addressed and forwarded, postage paid, for fifteen years. It took Grafton ten years from meeting the healer to stop drinking. Unlike the poet Gordon . . . who never stopped at all.

Three years before the jumper, when Grafton was fifteen, he would occasionally on a Saturday night buy a flagon or two of cheap McWilliams claret, sit on the grass in front of Gordon's grave and slowly, self-piteously drink himself into oblivion, quoting poems, often his own.

Grafton now thought it significant that he, a Church of England Melbourne son, was attracted to the grave of Gordon – a fellow pisspot – rather than all those others, divided by denomination into 'sections', that filled the grounds, including that terrible crook Sir Thomas Bent. Squizzy Taylor was also buried in Brighton Cemetery.

But this afternoon, not a Saturday, Grafton was not alone. Wearing his new jumper, he felt her wetness, lost himself in Marie's eyes. Like Gordon's, Grafton's complexion was pale; like the poet too he would be restless even in paradise. Being with Marie was not paradise, but it was close.

Born in the Portuguese Azores, descended from Scottish lairds and brought up in England, Gordon inherited strains from both his parents and possibly from farther back along the brilliant but chequered family line. A great talent, the poet manifested a curious imbalance between frantic action and a melancholy that marred his later life. Recklessly brave, he was given to frequent and unsteady repentance.

154

After being a mounted trooper, horse-breaker, member of the South Australian Parliament and then in the livery business at Ballarat, Gordon spent his final years at Brighton. Early in the mornings he swam in Port Phillip Bay, occasionally in the afternoons he walked into Melbourne to stop at the Yorick Club, or sat smoking his pipe in the office of Marcus Clarke's highly regarded *Colonial Monthly*, a publication that carried an increasing amount of his work. In 1867, Gordon's first book of poems, *Seaspray and Smoke Drift*, was published in Melbourne. Few books were printed, even fewer were read. In 1870, still training horses, famous as a daring steeple-chaser, honoured as a steward of the Melbourne Hunt Club, revered by Clarke and Henry Kendall, Gordon was putting the finishing touches to *Bush Ballads and Galloping Rhymes*. Despite widespread literary regard following publication of 'The Sick Stock-Rider', the poet was still in debt, but strongly hoped that a case being concluded in England would establish his claim to ancestral lands of the Gordons in Scotland and leave him free of financial problems.

As Marie mouthloved him, transporting him to that place where no light wearies and no love wanes, Grafton felt tall and powerful, a shining soul with syllables of fire. 'O Marie,' he sang as she, kneeling before him, in front of the column, brought him off. 'O Christ, O Holy Jesus, please don't go to England. Stay here with me. For ever.'

He stooped down to touch her head. 'That was wonderful. But I need a drink.' 'I don't,' she said with a smile, wet mouth, her lips moist and creamy.

The by-products of the gold rush had made Melbourne a pioneer in gas lighting, railways and electric telegraph. Privately-owned railway lines linked the city to outlying suburbs, including Brighton, then a thinly-populated borough of three thousand people. The houses stood among vacant lots, tea-tree scrub and grass paddocks; wealthy storekeepers were already building their Italianate mansions within sound of the sea. By the late 1860s the boom which caused prices to skyrocket, giving working people the opportunity to climb the economic and social ladder, was past. The influx of the 1850s had ended and thousands of immigrants from abroad or other states were drifting home. Melbourne's population was near to stagnation, business was depressed.

Armed with a flagon of claret on a Saturday night, edgy, empty and feeling utterly alone, Grafton when sixteen would often walk to the Brighton Cemetery. Drawn to Gordon's grave, he wolfed down the red as darkness fell. 'Do you give yourself to me *utterly*?' Grafton cried. He had just discovered Ezra Pound. 'Body and no body, flesh and no flesh, not as a fugitive blindly or bitterly, but as a child might with no other wish. Yes, *utterly*.' With wild enunciation the student hungrily drank. 'Then I will ferry you down to my estuary. And there I will bury you, lave you, and save you.' Grafton often got the words wrong. Drinking until he collapsed in a blackout, Grafton, gathering himself, stumbled home at 4 a.m. to his parents' Bill and Avis' neat South Caulfield home. As he entered Hancock Street, the suburban dawn looked like blood upon the wattle. That powerful symbol and forget-me-not of an Australia which the Poet Gordon – Scottish, alcoholic and estranged – had connected with this unfamiliar land into which Grafton had been born. An Australia that Grafton, under the influence of his history teacher at Forest Hill, had dimly begun to love.

Looking for cheap permanent lodgings to fit his straightened means, away from the city and close to the sea, Gordon found a brick and weatherboard cottage occupied by Hugh Kelly and his wife, No 10 Lewis Street, Brighton. It was about eight miles from Melbourne and a mile from the sands of Port Phillip Bay. Kelly was a gardener to the lawyer-politician

George Higinbotham, who had been Victorian Attorney General from 1863 to 1868 and was afterwards Chief Justice of Victoria ... Long after Gordon's death in 1870, a great many Victorians could recite his verses off by heart.

A long, lean youth, Grafton Everest had sharp features and green eyes with a very peculiar glitter. Also long and lean, Gordon had bushy, overhanging eyebrows. On casual acquaintance one would never consider him educated, as from long intercourse with rough people in the Bush he had picked up their manner of speaking.

Although Grafton had only begun drinking in fourth form, the odds against him were lengthening. Something in his personality responded powerfully to alcohol, despite the consequences.

Grafton's father never touched a drop. His grandfather had died an alcoholic. Once, in a rare display of vulnerability, his dad had confided that as a boy he had lost two bicycles looking for his father. Grafton thought that woefully sad.

In Brighton Gordon joined the volunteer Artillery Corps. He was issued a service rifle, although his eyesight made him an unpredictable marksman. Here he could make friends of a sort, wear the Queen's uniform and play at soldiering. He became a regular customer at the Marine Hotel, not the nearest to his home but the one he preferred. In the afternoons he walked to Melbourne and back, or took the train.

Although only thirty-six, physically and mentally he felt at the end of his tether. His health broken, in almost constant pain from riding injuries, he was bankrupt – unless his luck changed. Gordon's death-wish struggled with the old desire to get away from it all, to sail back to England and begin a new life, or to renew an old one. He was on the razor's edge.

After Marie left with her husband for England, Grafton continued at Monash, drinking even more heavily, Often he would walk from Avis' home with Shadow, his thin, black kelpie, to the Marine Hotel in Dendy Street. At the time he was not aware that the poet had drunk there, as much later had the pianist Percy Grainger – to fleetingly escape his maniacal mother Rose. But only lemonade. Percy kept his promise never to touch alcohol or tobacco as long as he lived. Once walking the wrong way home, Grafton spent the night with a tram conductor in the tea-tree by the beach near Park Street where an Aboriginal midden still remained. Shadow went back on his own. Sea spray and smoke drifting from the factories of Port Melbourne covered them both. The conductor lost his hat.

Sitting in the public bar of the Nottinghill Hotel after closing time with 'Commie George,' an ex-president of the Victorian Communist Party who had become worse for wear from drink, Grafton would write long and intimate letters to Marie telling, half-truthfully, how much he missed her and recounting, gratefully and graphically, what had occurred that late afternoon by Adam Lindsay Gordon's grave. Since the cemetery, most of his liaisons had been with men – commercial travellers, truck-drivers, an Anglican priest. Grafton wasn't fussy. Like the poet, Grafton returned relentlessly to alcohol only to find it aggravated his own already acute tendency to remorse, self-laceration and disgust.

He wrote to Marie sporadically for almost all of his third year at Monash, but his love letters elicited no response. Until one day in late November, just after his exams, Grafton received a parcel from Oxford, addressed care of his parents' home. All of his airletters, printed in his large, child-like hand, had been returned. On a plain sheet of paper was written precisely, in red: 'Never communicate with me or my wife again. G. Holmes.' Although he missed the thought of Marie and her mouth, Grafton did just that.

'I have not been well lately, I never got over that fall

and since then I have taken to drink. At least, I don't get drunk but I drink a good deal more than I ought to do for I have a good deal of pain in my head and back and I get so awfully low spirited and miserable that if I had a strong sleeping draught near me I'm afraid I might take it. I have carried one that I should never wake from – you will perhaps be very shocked old fellow to see me write in this strain but I am not exaggerating at least and if only I could persuade myself that I am a little mad I might do something of that sort. I really do feel a little mad at times and I begin to think that I have had more trouble than I can put up with. I could almost say more than I deserve, though this would probably be untrue.'

Self-pity touched with defiance meant that Grafton had few friends. Those who remained, although loyal, were themselves unstable. His intake of amphetamines and barbiturates, washed down with booze, rapidly increased. He had even been treated with LSD at the Alfred Hospital. The images he saw then were so terrifying he couldn't talk for a month. Grafton loathed being asked what he did and who he was, but in his heart, although he was not actually writing, Grafton usually thought of himself as 'a writer'.

Deeply despondent, Gordon came into Melbourne on 23 June 1870, the day of publication of *Bush Ballads*.

After Henry Kendall showed Gordon a proof of his review, they walked a long time in close communion on their gloomy fortunes, bidding each other what was to be a last farewell, at a neighbouring railway station.

Kendall lived in Fitzroy, not far from Collins Street, and Gordon called occasionally to recite or discuss poetry. His review had begun kindly, but Kendall did point to his fellow poet's 'inability to penetrate below the surface level of the tears of things'. Gordon did not take the train home from the nearest railway station; he walked to Flinders Street, where he saw his friend Mr Madden, MLA, who recollected:

. . . I met him a little after 4 o'clock on a winter's day
and walked with him as far as St Kilda. Of one thing
I am clear, that when I left him at St Kilda he was
absolutely sober, but very much depressed and
melancholy. He told me he had asked a friend to lend
him £100 to enable him to get to England, but his
friend had refused to make the advance and he was
most downhearted and despondent.

After having tea with Margaret – his wife – and
going to bed early, he left home before dawn. Carrying
his service rifle he walked to the Marine Hotel and
asked for the landlord, Mr Prendergast, whose son said
that he was still asleep. Gordon said not to wake him
and walked on towards the beach. On the way he
passed William Harrison, a fisherman who knew him
and nodded, but Gordon took no notice. At nine o'clock
William Allen, a storekeeper, was looking for his cow
in the thick tea-tree scrub which lined the sand when
he came upon the body of a man with a rifle lying by his
side, his head smashed open by a bullet. It was Gordon.

While she was half asleep, Maggie Gordon recalled
that she felt a kiss, but no more.

At night, Grafton would walk along the beach from
Elwood to Middle Brighton, and if he had not picked up
a stranger would spend the night on the pier or a little
further out, on the tiny lighthouse, drinking claret. He
would stay awake until dawn reciting 'Wynken,
Blynken and Nod,' abandoned to the lapping sea.

Grafton remembered that in first form at Gardenvale
Central Mrs Ball, a chain smoker, told class that seeds
from the wattle that stood above Gordon's grave were
distributed to school children for planting. Who would
have done such a wonderful thing? Surely it couldn't
have been the Brighton Town Clerk?

Craving for a drink, Grafton in the winter of his honours year woke up his supervisor Dr Noel Paterson at 5
a.m. on a Sunday morning at his shorefront Elwood flat

begging for a drink. Noel, tall, grey-haired and Anglo-Irish, now editor of *History Review*, gave him a bottle of port on condition he drank in the sand dunes. An hour later he was back for more. Grafton was never invited in again.

Bush Ballads and Galloping Rhymes had a print-run of 100 copies. When Henry Kendall's generally favourable review reached the streets in the morning of 25 June 1870 Gordon lay dead on the beach. Grafton thought of Gordon as this country's Brendan Behan. Mournfully he sang out loud: 'Australia has lost her sweet angry singer, no longer will his poems shine desire. We'll ring out in anguish our song through the night, for alas bold Gordon is dead.'

His eyesight was so bad that he could not see beyond the ears of his horse. He was probably drinking that night, but waited until early morning to take his rifle, kiss his sleeping wife and walk to Brighton beach where he placed the muzzle in his mouth.

In June 1870 Melbourne was in the midst of 'an epidemic of suicide'. The *Australasian* of 12 March 1870 had pointed to six recent attempts, four successful, and predicted more to come. The article speculated on causes, recognising psychological and physical motivations and also the effects of drinking, which it described as particularly dangerous because, 'the climate of these regions furnishes so powerful a stimulus to the nervous system'. A Mr Henry Walstab jumped, or perhaps merely fell, off the Brighton jetty while Gordon was preparing his own last journey to the beach. On the morning after the poet's death, the *Age* proclaimed 'the mania for suicide and murder is indeed upon us.'

Grafton lost track of Marie. He wrote off a stolen car by driving drunk without a licence off the Camden Bridge after being invited to give a paper at an Australian History conference at Menangle. Three months in hospital meant he had to repeat his finals. Testimony

161

from Professor Ian Staples coupled with the expertise of lawyer Jimmy Legge meant Grafton got off all charges with a suspended sentence. After scraping through his honours year with a 2A (he wrote a thesis on the English Civil War in a padded cell made into a temporary study in the Alfred Hospital), in 1967 Grafton got a job tutoring at the University of Queensland. By the time the year was up he had finished in Boggo Road jail, and gained the dubious distinction of being the only person, other than Gordon Childe – the distinguished Marxist anthropologist – ever sacked by the History Department at the University of Queensland. Childe 'leapt to his death' at Blackheath in the Blue Mountains, shortly after returning from overseas to do so.

Grafton's father Bill succumbed to a combination of heart and asthma attacks and Parkinson's. Grafton briefly returned to live with Avis until in February he wangled a Tutorship in History at the University of Western Australia – with an old teacher of his from Monash who had just been made professor. Grafton was also enrolled for a PhD – on the English anarchist William Godwin – but apparently no-one in Perth knew enough to supervise.

It took three days and nights to go by train from Melbourne to Perth – Grafton had never crossed the Nullarbor sober. Bombed out on booze and purple hearts the entire way, Grafton lost all his money to a Croat in a marathon pontoon and poker game and what remained of his honour to the drink waiter. All he had when he arrived at the Edwardian interstate station was a tiny suitcase which Avis had packed.

Grafton's brooding, excitable figure emerged half-drunk and dishevelled out of the train. Tall John Hunter, bearded then and a thorough Christian, was there to meet him. 'Good to see you,' said Professor Hunter, loyal as ever, as he briskly carried the solitary case. 'You'll be pleased to know that we've arranged a most suitable supervisor for your thesis. A Reverend Doctor Holmes. He's just arrived from Oxford. Where he's done a brilliant PhD himself, on Christian anarchism.'

His faithful friend, William Trainor, bought the plot next to Gordon's grave so that his bones might lie beside. Elizabeth Annie Bright, to whom Gordon was romantically attached, tended the graves of his daughter at Ballarat and his own at Brighton, carefully gathering seeds from a wattle tree over-hanging it and distributing them to school children to plant.

The following year Grafton Everest was having shock therapy in the Case Western Reserve Mental Hospital, Ohio. Two of his poems – both about misplaced love and suicide – appeared in A *Gathering of Sundays*, a collection from the Cleveland Poets Workshop. His girlfriend Rosemary had an abortion. Some time later in the same hospital Grafton was drinking gin out of a bottle, his back to those in the ward watching TV. 'Hey Aussie,' shouted a patient. 'The first guy in the world is about to walk on the moon.' 'Who gives a fuck about that,' responded Grafton. Had Christ appeared clad in a green watermelon, or Ghengis Khan ridden in from the steppes, Grafton would have offered the same response.

During his last week in Ohio, Grafton in defiant and resolute despair tried to kill himself with a huge overdose of sleepers. After being stomach-pumped he rang Rosie, begging her to bring in more tablets. Because she could not bear to see him suffer, because she loved him and thought there was no hope, because they shoot horses don't they, she did as she was asked and was caught at Reception with two bottles of Seconal. Rosemary was arrested; Grafton was deported. He joined Alcoholics Anonymous in 1971.

Remarkably Gordon, a true Christian, forgave Grafton his indiscretions. Marie and he even 'looked after' Grafton. Almost every Saturday they had him over to their Cottesloe home for a meal, usually a roast. To be fair, Grafton did amuse their twins – Cecilia and Frank – by singing such unlikely songs as 'Yummy, yummy, yummy, I've got love in my tummy' and 'I know a man who saw an Oo-poo-pa-doop.' When they were quiet he sang 'Barbara Allen'.

The poet was born in 1833. While Captain Gordon his father was relatively stable, mother Harriet was given to melancholic, religious obsessions and neurotic despair. She strongly disapproved of her son's inattention to schooling and that he mixed in the 'low company' of boxers, stable-hands and race-course urgers. Gordon was either 'expelled' or 'removed' from the Royal Military Academy at Woolwich in 1851. Of his early sexual activity little is known, although shortly before his departure to Australia in August 1853 he announced he had 'lost his heart' to a neighbouring farmer's daughter – Jane Bridges – to whom he unsuccessfully proposed. In an undated letter to his closest friend, Charley Walker, he boasted of a shipboard flirtation with a young married woman. He arrived in Adelaide in November 1853.

Why, Grafton wondered, did Gordon forgive? Perhaps he fancies me? Certainly his supervisor appeared to *look* at him in a peculiar way, especially after a few white wines. His tiny eyes glittered – with what Grafton could not quite determine . . . envy? or lust? or both?

Predictably, Grafton and Marie came together again – usually in the kitchen. But only for 'oral persuasion' as Grafton's old mate Broken-Hill Dick described it, after he had a prostate operation.

Dr Holmes, once a month, ran Saturday evening soirées at which a small group of nominally Christian academics, over mulled claret, would present papers on topics like 'Situational Ethics' and 'Christian Existentialism'. Gordon, thin and precise, chaired every session. Grafton would excuse himself, while Marie, who did not drink herself, would service him briefly but enthusiastically in the kitchen. Although she would never allow him to 'make love' properly, she would always swallow, her eyes wide opened. While she continued preparing savouries and supper, Grafton would return, wine-mug full, to hear the rest of the paper.

No-one was any wiser, and apparently no-one was hurt.

The University of Western Australia was not an unqualified success as Grafton spent more time in the Claremont Mental Hospital than he did in front of class. Also there was a scandal with a student in college. So Professor Hunter gently suggested that Grafton should leave. Fortunately, he had picked up a Fulbright to America and a graduate assistant-ship at a private university in Cleveland, Ohio. It wasn't Princeton, but it was academically okay. To the untutored eye Grafton still looked quite good on paper.

Gordon's proposal to Jane Bridges took her by surprise: 'I was just leaving (with my father) when Gordon came into the room ... and said ... abruptly, "I am going away and have come to say 'goodbye' ." I simply said "I am sorry you are going". Then, as by a lightning flash was revealed to me the beauty of a face which I had hitherto regarded as expressionless, for the lad had never looked straight into mine, and I knew that he was sensitive regarding his nearness of sight; at my words he flushed crimson and said, "One word from you and I will not go". At this moment I recall the look of entreaty which accompanied his brief confession and request. I intuitively knew what I had never before suspected, my heart seemed to leap into my throat – I awkwardly added, "We are all sorry, Mr Gordon, but I cannot say a word to induce you to stay after all the trouble and expense you have given your poor father". Then he said, "I will be and do all my father wishes if you will only say one word". Then I repeated, "I cannot.

Why have you said nothing of this before?" He said,
"Because I was afraid you would ridicule or shun me,
and I could not have stood it," and added, "I shall hope
unless there is another; is there another?" I felt obliged
to say "Yes, there is another!" Then the crimson flush
died out of the beautiful face, and tears gushed into my
eyes.'

His last day in Perth, Grafton arranged to meet
Marie in his sleeper on the train, after Professor
Hunter had bade him farewell. She was very fond of
him, Marie explained. But she was also very fond of
Gordon. And she was his wife. But she liked doing what
she did to Grafton. She liked doing it a lot. Marie was a
Christian of the most compassionate sort. 'I'd like you
to be my friend. And I won't do this with anyone else. I
never have,' she said looking deeply with her oceanic
eyes. 'Not even with Gordon – he wouldn't approve.' 'I
can accept that,' said Grafton unbuttoning himself.

Dr Holmes burst into the cabin. 'How could you?' he
said, looking directly at Grafton and smacking Marie
across the head. 'After all I've done.' Tears in their
eyes, supervisor and wife left the cabin. 'I'll never see
you again,' cried Marie. 'But I don't feel ashamed. I
don't.'

'I need a drink' said Grafton, pouring a sherry. 'Why
is life so complicated? Why does this always happen?'
He began reciting:

> 'I – knowing the course was foolish
> And guessing the goal was pain,
> Stupid, and stubborn and mulish,
> Followed and follow again.

'Perhaps I should write a poem myself.'

On 4 August 1933, the centenary of his birth, The
Times announced that Gordon was to have a memorial
in the Poet's Corner, Westminster Abbey.

Grafton learned years later – after he returned

from America – that Marie had gone blind. Was it hysterical blindness, he wondered. It seemed so unfair.

Surely Brother Mandus could have intervened?

Grafton tried in vain to track her down. The Reverend Doctor Holmes had, it appeared, taught in Tasmania then vanished into thin air. The academic community in Australia was small but Grafton, despite his persistence, could find no trace. Eventually he gave up trying, until one day he read in the Age that Gordon had been killed by a bus in the Sudan. Marie wasn't mentioned. Sometimes, late at night, sober and insomniac, Grafton missed her desperately.

I feel like an exile, he thought. Just like Lindsay Gordon. At least, I stopped drinking. Arthritis and stomach problems caused him considerable pain. He attended AA five nights a week.

'Tally-ho' Thompson, an English hunting friend, remembered Gordon as 'Mucker' because of his tendency to run amok.

Grafton was forty. After seeing Avis, nearly blind, still in her South Caulfield home, Grafton, fourteen and a half stone, weary, restless and married, stopped off on his way to Tullamarine. He went again to the poet's grave. The wattle had long gone. Grafton, now a parent, noticed for the first time an inscription for Gordon's daughter: 'Annie Lindsay Gordon died at Ballarat in 1868 aged 11 months. And was reinterred in 1919.' Poor little mite cried Grafton, lamenting mainly for himself. She died only two years before the Poet shot himself.

Peeking to make sure no-one was looking, Grafton knelt by the tomb, touching the small patch of grass, and prayed.

'Well, Adam, I know you didn't stop drinking. You probably know that, unlike your own good self, I'm off all booze and pills. But I'm stuck in Brisbane. Been there for nine years in January. When I told a mate from Sydney that, he said "Jesus, you'd get less for manslaughter".

'So, Adam, I would be grateful if you'd get me a job in Sydney. It's a lectureship in Australian history. I'd like to be given tenure as well. Okay? But most of all I want to stay sober. And Adam, I'd be grateful if you could let me write a bit and take away this dreadful pain. I just don't know how long I can hang on. So, old Adam, do what you can.

'I know it is probably asking a bit much, but although I want to stay married I wouldn't mind a little bit of romance.'

Grafton left a wildflower by the broken column and, tears in his eyes, lumbered towards the gate in Hawthorn Road. A weary wayfarer and far from home, he hailed a cab.

'Do you see the brightest star in all the skies?' pointed Avis when Grafton was five years old. 'That's your brother Rodney.'

'Why do we, I wonder?' Grafton asked the Jewish cab driver as they passed by Princes Park where in the summer of 1959 a pock-marked tram conductor with face lines like W. H. Auden told him, a schoolboy, that he looked like a writer. Grafton had never forgotten it, or him. Why do we ceaselessly search for love in forms it never takes, in places it can never be?'

'You've got such problems,' reflected the driver lighting up and speaking about his own divorce. 'Why do we survive at all?'

After Gordon's death, Maggie worked for three years as a seamstress. Then she married another Scot, Peter Low. Brought to Australia in 1852 as a child of eight, he worked as a shepherd and shearer until he joined the Survey Department. The 'ever-delicate' Maggie, barely five feet high, contentedly raised three daughters and four sons. Their house was plastered with pictures and mementos of Gordon, like a shrine. She died in 1919 aged seventy-four.

Alone, suffering and deeply depressed with the routine and monotony of middle-aged, working life, Grafton nodded and slowly got out of the taxi. I've got to *escape*. Huge in his despair, Grafton stood brooding over his large suitcase.

As the light dimmed outside and the loud speaker made a final call for Flight 1203, he started the long walk towards the dark tower.

'I beleave I was the last known man to see the poet on that fatal morning and the first to find him on the beach at the bottom of Park Street and I think the first to break the sad news to his wife. I was twenty-two years of age and was with a Mr Bignall Baker. We were looking over the fence shaken in a sea breeze, when the Poet passed with his reifel and remarked the fact that Gordon was out so early a little after six am, I felt it curious and said so as the Butts was quite the other side of Brighton ... I saw him go to the door of the Moreen [i.e. Marine] Hotel which had not yet opened, he knocked and was admitted. I still watched – in some five minutes I saw him come out and go down Park Street – shortly after a Scot Alen Grosse whose business place was opposite rushed in and said he was looking for his cow in the tea-tree on the beach and he came across a man who apperantly had shot himself. I concluded and jumped on a horse and galloped down ... Yes it was Gordon, just on the left of the beach as I rode down Park Street, there lay our Poet with the reifel laying on him, his hat by his side, a pipe knife and tobacco inside. I saw where he had broken a bow from a tree, the forked stick he had made out of it. He was laying with his head up hill, and reifel butt between his feet, and sun where the bullet had passed through the top of his head and hit in its transit the very tree he had broken the branch from – others then came along, I then hastened to break the sad news to his wife.'

> Question not, but live and labour,
> Till yon goal be won,

Helping every feeble neighbour,
Seeking help from none,
Life is mostly froth and bubble,
Two things stand like stone –
Kindness in another's trouble,
Courage in your own.

THE END

Pushed from the Wings
by Ross Fitzgerald

'Like Queensland politics, the book is funny in bits but mostly
offensive'
JOHN SHAW

Ross Fitzgerald's first novel, PUSHED FROM THE
WINGS, is a riotously funny black comedy set in a
Queensland of the very near future. His teetotal
hypochondriac hero, Grafton Everest, is destined to become
a late twentieth century Australian legend: an Antipodean
early middle-age mix of Walter Mitty, Billy Liar and Sandy
Stone. An anti-hero of outrageous proportions.

'The novel's rough mix of intelligence and spleen
demonstrates something more than a mere talent to offend'
CARL HARRISON-FORD, NATIONAL TIMES

'Grafton Everest is triumphantly repugnant'
STEVE J. SPEARS

'Grafton Everest is brilliantly revolting'
THOMAS SHAPCOTT

0 552 99338 7

BLACK SWAN

The Cider House Rules
John Irving

'Bound to make as vivid an impression as The World According to Garp' said *Publishers Weekly* of John Irving's magnificent new novel spanning six decades.

Set among the apple orchards of rural Maine, it is a perverse world in which Homer Wells' odyssey begins. As the oldest unadopted offspring at St Cloud's orphanage, he learns about the skills which, in one way or another, help young and not-so-young women, from Wilbur Larch, the orphanage's founder, a man of rare compassion and with an addiction to ether.

Dr. Larch loves all his orphans, especially Homer Wells. It is Homer's story we follow, from his early apprenticeship in the orphanage surgery, to his adult life running a cider-making factory and his strange relationship with the wife of his closest friend.

'John Irving has been compared with Kurt Vonnegut and J. D. Salinger, but is arguably more inventive than either. Wry, laconic, he sketches his characters with an economy that springs from a feeling for words and mastery over his craft. This superbly original book is one to be read and remembered'
THE TIMES

'The Cider House Rules is difficult to define and impossible not to admire'
DAILY TELEGRAPH

'Like the rest of Irving's fiction, it is often disconcerting, but always exciting and provoking'
THE OBSERVER

0 552 99204 6

BLACK SWAN

The Water Method Man
by John Irving

'John Irving, it is abundantly clear, is a true artist. He is not
afraid to take on great themes.'
LOS ANGELES TIMES

An hilarious novel about a man with a complaint more
serious than Portnoy's, *The Water-Method Man* is a
work of consummate artistry, bizarre imagery and sharp
social and psychological observation, by an author whose
original brilliance has already placed him in the front
rank of contemporary American writers.

'Brutal reality and hallucination, comedy and pathos. A rich,
unified tapestry . . . something of beauty'
TIME

0 552 99207 0

BLACK SWAN

Redback
Howard Jacobson

'It was just my luck to get bitten by a Redback.
'There's no such thing as luck,' Gunnar McMurphy used to
say. 'You chose to sit where you sat. A bite is a transaction
between two parties — a biter and a biteree. You sat in wait
for that spider with every bit as much purpose as he sat in
wait for you.'
'It wasn't a he — it was a she. Only the shes are venomous.'

The biteree in question is Karl Leon Forelock, product of
the Northern English town of Partington (the wettest spot
in Europe) and a graduate with a double starred first in
the Moral Decencies from Malapert College, Cambridge.
Sent to Sydney on a CIA bursary, in order to teach the
Australians how to live, Leon Forelock soon discovers that
there are those amongst the native population who believe
that they have an education to pass on in return. But it is
at the hands of the women of Australia that Leon receives
his most painful, and on occasions his most pleasurable,
lessons. Meanwhile, in a foul, dilapidated bush privy, way
up in the Bogong High Plains, the Redback sucks her teeth
and waits her turn . . .

Redback is further proof that Howard Jacobson, author of
Coming from Behind and *Peeping Tom* is the most
devastatingly funny novelist writing in English today.

'A heady, jangly, clever, priapic riot'
EVA TUCKER, HAMPSTEAD & HIGHGATE EXPRESS

'Confirms there is no more original comic writer in Britain'
MICHAEL LEAPMAN, SOUTHSIDE

'Jacobson has no trouble in making us laugh with him —
although the reader often has to duck the spittle'
NICHOLAS SHAKESPEARE, THE TIMES

'An outrageously gifted funny man'
CHRISTOPHER WORDSWORTH, THE GUARDIAN

0 552 99252 6

BLACK SWAN

God Knows
Joseph Heller

'Mr Heller is dancing at the top of his form again . . .
original, sad, wildly funny and filled with roaring'
MORDECAI RICHLER, NEW YORK TIMES BOOK REVIEW

Joseph Heller's powerful, wonderfully funny, deeply moving
novel is the story of David — yes, *that* David: warrior king
of Israel, husband of Bathsheba, father of Solomon, slayer
of Goliath, and psalmist nonpareil . . . as well as the David
we've never known before now: David the cocky Jewish
kid, David the fabulous lover, David the plagiarised poet,
David the Jewish father, David the (one-time) crony of
God . . .

At last, David is telling is own story, and he's holding nothing
back — equally unembarrassed by his faults, his sins, his
prowess, his incomparable glory . . .

God Knows is an ancient story, a modern story, a love
story. It is a novel about growing up and growing old, about
men and women, about fathers and sons, about man and
God. It is a novel of emotional force, imaginative richness,
and unbridled comic invention. It is quintessential Heller.

'Joseph Heller is the outstandingly clever ideas-man of
modern fiction . . . brilliantly inventive'
JONATHAN RABAN, SUNDAY TIMES

'The unforgiving genius still flares, and the book is worth
the price of admission for the first few pages alone'
MARTIN AMIS, THE OBSERVER

0 552 99169 4

BLACK SWAN

A SELECTED LIST OF FINE NOVELS
AVAILABLE FROM BLACK SWAN

The prices shown below were correct at the time of going to press. However Transworld Publishers reserve the right to show new retail prices on covers which may differ from those previously advertised in the text or elsewhere.

☐	99348 4	**SUCKING SHERBET LEMONS**	*Michael Carson*	£3.99
☐	99228 3	**A FINE EXCESS**	*Jane Ellison*	£3.95
☐	99338 7	**PUSHED FROM THE WINGS**	*Ross Fitzgerald*	£3.99
☐	99327 1	**VINEGAR SOUP**	*Miles Gibson*	£3.95
☐	99169 4	**GOD KNOWS**	*Joseph Heller*	£3.95
☐	99195 3	**CATCH-22**	*Joseph Heller*	£4.95.
☐	99208 9	**THE 158lb. MARRIAGE**	*John Irving*	£3.95
☐	99204 6	**THE CIDER HOUSE RULES**	*John Irving*	£3.95
☐	99209 7	**THE HOTEL NEW HAMPSHIRE**	*John Irving*	£4.95
☐	99206 2	**SETTING FREE THE BEARS**	*John Irving*	£4.95
☐	99207 0	**THE WATER METHOD MAN**	*John Irving*	£4.95
☐	99205 4	**THE WORLD ACCORDING TO GARP**	*John Irving*	£4.95
☐	99141 4	**PEEPING TOM**	*Howard Jacobson*	£3.95
☐	99063 9	**COMING FROM BEHIND**	*Howard Jacobson*	£3.95
☐	99252 6	**REDBACK**	*Howard Jacobson*	£3.95
☐	99243 7	**CONFESSIONS OF A FAILED SOUTHERN LADY**	*Florence King*	£3.99
☐	99337 9	**SOUTHERN LADIES AND GENTLEMEN**	*Florence King*	£3.99
☐	99323 9	**DREAMS OF LEAVING**	*Rupert Thompson*	£4.95
☐	99130 9	**NOAH'S ARK**	*Barbara Trapido*	£2.95
☐	99056 6	**BROTHER OF THE MORE FAMOUS JACK**	*Barbara Trapido*	£3.95

ORDER FORM

All these books are available at your bookshop or newsagent, or can be ordered direct from the publishers. Just tick the titles you want and fill in the form below.
   Corgi/Bantam Books,
   Cash Sales Department,
   P.O. Box 11, Falmouth, Cornwall TR10 9EN.

Please send a cheque or postal order (no currency) and allow 60p for postage and packing for the first book plus 25p for the second book and 15p for each additional book ordered up to a maximum charge of £1.90 in UK.

B.F.P.O. customers please allow 60p for the first book, 25p for the second book plus 15p per copy for the next 7 books, thereafter 9p per book.

Overseas customers, including Eire, please allow £1.25 for postage and packing for the first book, 75p for the second book, and 28p for each subsequent title ordered.

NAME (Block Letters)...

ADDRESS ....

....

Ross Fitzgerald was born in Melbourne and gained his PhD in political science at the University of New South Wales. Since 1977 he has taught at Griffith University in Brisbane.

Dr Fitzgerald is well-known on Australian television and radio as a political and social commentator. He is the editor of numerous books on politics, the author of *The Eyes of the Angels*, a collection of poems, and of a best-selling two-volume history of Queensland, *From the Dreaming to 1915* and *From 1915 to the Early 1980's.*

Author photograph by Greg Newington

Also by Ross Fitzgerald
PUSHED FROM THE WINGS

and published by Black Swan